Waking Nightmare...

Her niece, Alice, was crouched by a tidal pool as Phoebe lay back and closed her eyes. After the few hours' sleep last night, a nap would be heaven. Her mind wandered over the black-and-white body on the stones of the harbor. She fell asleep wondering just what or who would do that to an orca.

Dark night. Dark waves. Dark whale. She was alone, cutting through the water in search of her pod, powerful tail sending her forward like a torpedo, breath coming in powerful bursts from her blowhole. She had to go faster because something was coming. Something was after her, big and dark and powerful that stole the stars from the sky, blocked the light of the moon. It shook the world around her and stole all the breath from her lungs. A blow and she was dying, fighting to stay afloat, to live, to protect her unborn calf.

"Aunt Bee? Are you all right?"

Her eyes opened on blue and for a moment she couldn't remember where she was. Wind in her hair. Sun on her face. *She should be in the principal's office, convincing him he was wrong. They had to do something instead of sitting in her office.*

"Aunty Bee?" The worry in the voice brought her up to sitting and she blinked to steady herself. Not an office. A beach. And she was—her eyes flickered from her niece, who should be three thousand miles away with her mother, and then locked on the kayaks beside her. Kayaking with Alice. Right. She scrubbed her face.

"My goodness, that was a nightmare. I dreamed I was Light Fin and something killed me."

Alice was looking at her with concern in her eyes. She held something in her palm, but she closed her hand and shoved it in her pocket. "You—you're okay now, though, right?"

Was she? She felt shaky as heck and weaker than she'd felt since... well... since she'd gone off work.

"I—I tried to wake you. I shook you. You still didn't wake. I—I finally slapped you. I'm sorry."

Alice's concern had melted to reveal an underlay of visceral fear. The poor kid was on a beach three thousand miles from home and the only adult she knew had gone terribly wonky.

BOOKS BY THE AUTHOR

Mystery
(Written as K.L. Abrahamson):
Phoebe Clay Mysteries
Through Deep Water

The Detektiv Kazakov Mysteries
After Yekaterina
Mareson's Arrow
The Tsarina's Mask
Ivan's Wolf

Aung And Yamin Mysteries
Death by Effigy
Death in Passing
Death in Umber

Fantasy:
The Cartographer Universe (in chronological order)
The Warden of Power

The Cartographer's Daughter

The American Geological Survey Series:
Afterburn
Aftershock
Aftermath
Afterimage

Terra Incognita
Terra Infirma
Terra Nueva

THROUGH
DARK WATER

K.L. Abrahamson

Twisted Root Publishing

Through Dark Water
Copyright © 2015 Karen L. Abrahamson
All rights reserved, including the right of reproduction, in whole or in part in any form.

Published 2015 by Twisted Root Publishing

Book and cover design © Twisted Root Publishing
Cover image: © Daniel Barnes|iStock.com

ISBN: 978-1-927753-48-4

This book is licensed for your personal enjoyment only. All rights are reserved. This book is a work of fiction. Names, characters, places and incidents are the product of the author's imagination or are used fictitiously. Any resemblance to actual events, locales, or persons, living or dead, is coincidental. This book, or parts thereof, may not be reproduced in any form without permission.

If you purchase this book without a cover you should be aware that this book may have been stolen property and reported as "unsold and destroyed" to the publisher. In such a case neither the author nor the publisher has received any payment for this "stripped book".

**Dedicated to Jolene and Barb,
the real Alice and Becca.**

Acknowledgements:

Many thanks to Marcelle Dube for her excellence as a first reader; Colleen Kuehne for her sharp-eyed editing; and M.D. Abrahamson for her proofing. Thanks as well to Kim, Lennie and Alena who helped make kayaking in Johnstone Strait a learning experience.

THROUGH
DARK WATER

K.L. Abrahamson

Chapter 1

It was dark out—black in the campground—the only light coming from the humming fluorescent fixture over the washroom outbuilding door. Phoebe Clay stood under the canopy of dripping, old growth cedar, hemlock and spruce and tried very hard to ignore that light. etective Kazakov were too harsh, too stark. Too reminiscent of things in her past she would prefer not to remember. Nope, the almost total dark of the mostly uninhabited northeast coast of Vancouver Island was scary, but it was also a thick blanket that she could use to hide from so many things. Like Rick.

Around her in the chilly dark there were other campers stirring from the half-seen RVs and trailers scattered among the huge trees and the light brush of huckleberry bush, salal, and fern. Mostly the other campers were fishermen up early for a day chasing salmon in the northern Pacific waters. There were no other crazy fools like her in a tent.

She unlocked her Subaru that hunkered down beside the campsite and pulled a Coleman stove and breakfast supplies out onto the night-damp picnic table. A couple of matches later and she had a hissing propane burner going and water heating to brew coffee. Beyond the sounds of the campers stirring came the distant low rumble of ocean surf. The Inside Passage up the western coast of North America was ready and waiting just a stone's throw away—if she could get her niece, Alice, up out of her sleeping bag.

"Come on, kiddo," she said. "We've got to get moving if we want to get our pick of kayaks for the day."

It was an early July morning and Phoebe stuck her head into the blue, three-man, domed tent where Alice, her twelve-year-old niece, had performed another face plant onto her sleeping bag. The girl was still in her sleeping t-shirt and underwear, though she *had* managed to pull socks on. A little progress, then, but a groan was all Phoebe got in response, from somewhere under the mop of blonde hair that hid Alice's face. That and a snuffle that was suspiciously like a snore in counterpoint to the sound of the ocean.

"You make me come in there and you're not going to be happy," Phoebe sing-songed. To demonstrate, she reached in and tickled a sock-foot. In a sudden sign of life, the foot yanked away like a kid trying to hide a note in class, and then a single eye peered up at her through the matted curls, capturing what little light there was.

"But it's cold out there. And wet. And I hardly slept last night."

"Tell me about it. All your tossing and turning and complaining didn't make my sleep any easier either. But I want to see whales. I thought you did, too. So you've got five minutes to get yourself in gear and get out here for breakfast or I'm eating it all and leaving you here all day with rocky sleeping arrangements for company."

Alice groaned and dramatically covered her eyes with her arm. Phoebe turned her back on the tent and poured boiling water through filtered coffee and then poured a cup and sipped. Hot. Strong. Good. She clutched the steaming red mug between both hands to keep her fingers from freezing. This early in the morning it *was* flipping cold. A chill morning fog clung to the campground under the trees. Their thick branches tangled overhead with moss and ocean mist. It was morning, but dawn had yet to find the space under the trees. The darkness had lifted some, though. Instead of half-perceived points of movement, people were now sinister specters around the campground.

Most of the camp's fifty spaces were taken up with expensive RVs and trailers hauled by powerful pickups. Her little Subaru SUV looked like a pretender amongst all that metal and steel. The otherworldly glow of mist-diffused electric lights now came from inside those trailers and motorhomes as more people woke. The scents of bacon and eggs and omelets filled the air with enticements, along with the low drone of a morning news station reporting on the latest missing girl in the string of disappearances that had occurred along the Northern Vancouver Island highway. There'd been no bodies found yet. So much for happiness in the world.

She was glad she and Alice had run away for a little while. She turned back to the little Coleman stove, wondering why people would chose to bring the big bad world with them. It wasn't her idea of a holiday—nor of how she wanted to enjoy her first days of retirement. Not that freezing her butt off on a chilly morning was, either, but for the chance to see live killer whales close up and personal in the wild, she'd do it. After a career of placing order on the bedlam of her classrooms, it was time to put some adventure back into her life.

Sighing, she held her hands over the stove, then dug four eggs out of their supplies and a bowl and frying pan. Now if Alice would just get her butt in gear.

It was thanks to her habitual over-planning that she had breakfast makings at all. She'd brought the stove and groceries as a last minute decision to be prepared for the worst—something she'd learned to do in twenty-five years in the classroom. She'd mistakenly thought that Pirate Cove, the highly publicized and picturesque resort and jumping-off spot to salmon fishing, killer whale viewing, and the famous Robson Bight would provide some amenities. Instead, the place was in reality no more than a campground and string of three-hundred-dollar-a-night cottages that were set up for the fishing and whale watching tours that ran out of the harbor. The restaurants weren't open early enough to buy a hot breakfast for her and Alice before a day spent exploring and getting a feel for the water before the official whale watching kayak trip they would join tomorrow.

A rustling sound came from behind her and finally two socked and sandaled feet stuck out of the blue nylon tent followed by slim legs in black leggings and a grumbling girl in a blue Gore-Tex jacket.

"Geeze. It's still dark out."

"It's lighter than it was a few minutes ago. We get out from under these trees and it'll be daylight."

"What time is it?" Alice asked, fists grinding at the sleep still in her eyes. It was a movement she'd had ever since she was a baby and one that still stole Phoebe's heart. Sometimes she could still see that innocent toddler staring out at her from this moody preteen body—or the precious infant that her mother and Phoebe's sister, Becca, had brought home from the hospital.

Alice scowled up at her. "The time?"

Well, maybe make that *challenging young woman*. And stubborn. And demanding. All the things that had had Becca asking over and over whether Phoebe was *sure* she wanted to take Alice with her on her first après-retirement adventure.

Phoebe lifted her chin at the concrete washroom building fifty feet away. Its flickering white light glared through the hazy mist around the door. "It's six-thirty. Go get washed up. I'll have breakfast ready when you get back."

Still grumbling, Alice stood, zipped the tent behind her, and headed over to the amenities. Phoebe settled on the picnic table's damp bench, sipping coffee, and turned on the second Coleman burner; the scent of propane tanged the air. Butter melted in the battered frying pan on the blue-flamed burner while she broke and whipped the eggs into a bowl. When Alice emerged from the washroom, she poured the eggs into the sizzling butter and stirred. Pulling the coffeepot off the other burner, she fished a couple of slices of bread from a bag and set the bread on the flame to toast.

By the time Alice returned, scrub-faced and with her still-matted hair pushed behind her ears, Phoebe was stirring almost fully cooked eggs and had two pieces of only semi-charred toast. She grabbed two paper plates—all she had for dishes—and shared out the food. "Eat up. It'll warm you up. There's apple juice in a juice box if you want one."

"I want coffee. It's hot."

Not what she'd expect a twelve-year-old to drink. "Does your mother let you drink coffee?"

"Sometimes." Alice shrugged and Phoebe sighed. The kid was born into the Starbucks age where twelve-year-olds were sucking back peppermint lattes; she might not agree but she poured her a cup. Handed it to her. "This morning only. I will not have your mother saying I corrupted her daughter, you hear? And by the way, there's no milk. Or sugar."

She smiled to herself when Alice stared at the cup like it was from outer space.

Alice sipped, made a face, but the heat in the cup must have overcome her disgust. She tucked into the food and didn't even mention the charred toast—fresh air somehow burned away youthful fussiness even when coupled with lack of sleep. Or maybe it was the promise of whales. When they were done, the stove and supplies cleaned and packed away in the car, they headed out together. The light had increased and the mist had dissipated some—now it simply hovered in the branches overhead like a memory just out of reach. Around them the campground echoed with the sounds of voices—fishermen and women heading down to the pier and their waiting charter boats. The whale watching boats wouldn't be out until a more livable hour.

Thankfully, the food seemed to have revived the spirit of adventure in Alice. She hopped over the puddles like a kid, then remembered herself and fell back to Phoebe's more sedate pace.

"This is going to be fun, right?"

"It is."

"And we'll see whales?" Alice's big blue eyes were even bigger than normal in her fine-boned face—if that were possible. She was still a sylph of a girl who had inherited her mother's slim build as opposed to Phoebe's more solid construction. It was always strange how children went through a transitional purgatory between childhood and teenagerhood, when they were neither fish nor fowl, instead threading through those years in the middle with a foot in each world.

"We should. Like the brochure said, there are resident whales here. That's why all the tourists come here. Even Jacques Cousteau said it was pretty amazing."

"Who?" Alice looked the question at her, and Phoebe felt even more her age: fifty-five and she had already lived over half of her life. Now she was just on the downhill slide.

She sighed. "A marine biologist and oceanographer. He did a whole series of TV shows on the wonders of the underwater world." God save her from the terminally young.

Alice grabbed her hands and burst out laughing. "I know who he is, Aunt Bee. Mom hauled his shows up off of YouTube and made me watch them along with a zillion other things before I left to come here." She giggled. "You should have seen your face—like you thought you were so incredibly out of touch or something."

Still chuckling, she settled beside Phoebe; at twelve, her stride was already almost as long as her aunt's even though she hadn't reached her full growth. Where Phoebe was a solid five feet eight, Alice was only about five feet six, but the kid was all leg and had all the signs that she was entering another growth spurt. Given her dad was six feet four, she was likely going to be taller than her aunt by a long shot.

The briny scent of seaweed and the sound of surf met them as they rounded the corner from the campground and reached the tiny enclave of Pirate Cove. It spread before them, its ice cream colored clapboard buildings clinging for dear life to the backdrop of mist-draped cedar. Low marine clouds covered the sky, but wind off the water was stripping the clouds away and hints of blue shone through.

The water of the little bay was mostly smooth, the wind sending lazy, black, one foot swells curving onto the gravel shore. A lot of the buildings weren't even built on land. Instead they sat precariously on boardwalks that strung out along the high bank shore on water-grayed pilings that were thick with mussels. At the far end of the boardwalk sat a warehouse-sized building painted rust red that glowered across the water. In the early 1900s, a prosperous salmon cannery and lumber mill had thrived in the town. Those businesses had been replaced by tourism and now a portion of the old cannery housed a Killer Whale Interpretive Center that Phoebe intended to visit before they were done.

They walked down slope toward the boat launch where they were supposed to pick up their kayaks and a packed lunch arranged through Pirate Cove Resort, but though the kayaks were there, their bright colors slashing the monochrome morning grey, no one else was. Instead a string of apparently abandoned trucks with fiberglass fishing boats on trailers stood in a line waiting to launch, while a silent crowd had formed halfway along the shoreline's narrow tidal flats underneath the boardwalk pilings. The wind curling around the bay ruffled Phoebe's short gray-blonde hair, but brought the stink of something...dead. She recognized the scent from her nightmares.

Long dead, by the eye-watering stench of it.

Alice covered her nose with her hand. "What *is* that?"

"Something unusual by the look of it." And judging by the crowd, something that drew attention despite the smell. "Shall we go see?"

Nose still wrinkled against the stink, Alice looked between the kayaks and the crowd. "There's no one here to give us our kayaks anyway." She shrugged and led off down the boat launch and around onto the narrow beach between the water and the steep bank of the cove. Her bright blue jacket was a happy counterpoint to the grey morning.

Water lapped through the treacherous stones under their feet as they slipped and slid across the seaweed-slimed stone and driftwood. Among the barnacle-embossed stones were small colonies of sea anemone and large purple sea stars. The boardwalk was ahead and if the tide was fully in, they'd be walking knee-deep in water. The crowd of about twenty people had gathered under the pilings, a mix of the drab working fishermen's colors of the locals with a few bright splashes of designer Gore-Tex that clearly marked visitors to the cove. But regardless of the rancid smell, the way they huddled together said something was seriously wrong.

Phoebe slowed and caught Alice's shoulder. "Stay back here a moment while I check it out."

Alice glanced up with teenaged resentment in her eyes—one of those moments.

"Just do it because I'm your favorite aunt, okay?"

"You're my only aunt."

"So that should make me extra special."

Alice sighed as only a teenager could.

Leaving Alice a few steps away from the crowd, Phoebe reached the gathered people in the shadow of the boardwalk. Water splatted her head in a sad, briny rain from the mussels and seaweed that covered the pilings.

The people were strangely quiet—almost funereal. Whispers hissed between those at the rear of the gathering and someone closer to the center was sobbing, but mostly the people were strangely respectful.

"What's happened?" Phoebe asked softly, coming up between a man who clearly was a local, wearing a gray-green mackinaw and jeans, and a rangy young man with freckles and a quick smile who looked like he could be the older man's son. The older man had a thatch of sun-and-salt-faded brown hair, weathered lines around clear blue eyes, and clearly looked uncomfortable at what was happening. The younger one didn't yet have his father's breadth of shoulders, but he shared the older man's blue eyes. He just looked interested.

"A death in the family, I guess you could say," the older man said. "One of the whales. Going to be a pall over the tour boats today." He shook his head.

The crunch of footfall over the stones behind her turned Phoebe around. Another man pushed past Alice. He was tall, official looking and wore a shockingly bright red jacket and pressed jeans.

"Bert." The newcomer nodded at the man Phoebe had been speaking to. "What've we got?"

"One of the whales," Bert said and tipped his head toward the center of the crowd.

"Dead?" asked the newcomer.

"O' course dead. Can't you smell it?" Bert said.

The newcomer pushed through the people and they parted like butter, revealing three people at the center of the crowd standing beside a huge black-and-white body that had rolled broadside onto shore. It lay half on its side, the massive black dorsal fin sagging against the steep bank of the cove. Killer whale. Orca.

In the gravel and seaweed, it was so unlike the majestic animals she'd come to see that it could have been a fake covered in white and black neoprene rubber. But it wasn't. A blond-haired man in a blue jacket almost the same color as Alice's knelt at the front of the body, examining the bottle-nosed head. Where its eyes should be were just red sockets, as if something had eaten out its eyes. Something was wrong with its mouth, though she couldn't figure out what. A woman with dark hair pulled back in a ponytail and wearing the same colored blue jacket stood beside the man. She was the source of the sobbing.

At the other end of the body stood a youngish man—eighteen or nineteen, maybe—still feeling the weight of new-come adulthood. His hands were stuffed in his pockets and he glared resentment at her so hard that she almost left right there and then. Didn't he like the fact that people were staring at the whale or was something else the problem?

The boy was tall, clearly Aboriginal, black hair worn long over the collar, with high cheekbones and narrow face that suggested a heritage that might harken back to great plains tribes rather than the coastal nations. When he looked away, his black gaze locked on the body of the whale as if he could not believe it was here.

"Jeezus," the red-clad newcomer said, stopping beside the man at the carcass's head. "Do something, Wilbur. That damn thing is going to stink up the entire village. You think people are going to want a meal with this blowing in their faces?"

The blond-haired man stood up from examining the whale's mouth, his face pale. He was tall—taller than the newcomer—and had none of the manicured look of the latter. He had a weathered face, and she pegged him at about forty years old, like the man next to her, but something about the thoughtfulness of his face suggested he was no fisherman.

"So just what would you like me to do, Sam? Blow her up like the fools did with that humpback down south?" said the man named Wilbur. "We could spread rotting whale meat all over this village if you like."

"Who are they?" she murmured to Bert, the fisherman.

"That's John Wilbur of the Whale Interpretive Center," Bert, volunteered. "He's a marine biologist who keeps track of the whale population or some such. The woman's his assistant, Ayisha Meredith. She's doing her PhD or something. Both of them whale crazy, you might say. The guy in the red jacket is Sam Rayburn, the resort owner. He basically owns everything in Pirate Cove, including the Whale Interpretive Center building. This is my son, Donnie. I'm Bert. Bert Clarke."

"Phoebe Clay." She nodded and waved Alice forward. "My niece, Alice. It's a dead orca, Ali. You sure you want to see?"

Of course she did. Kids were fascinated by death. Using her smaller size, she weaseled her way forward to the front of the crowd. Phoebe trailed after her until they stood at the inner circle of bystanders.

"Well, you can't leave it here. It has to be moved straightaway. Couldn't we just tie a rope to it and drag it out to sea?" said the manicured Sam.

John Wilbur's hands flexed as if he was restraining himself. "'Fraid not, Sam. This is A39, one of the resident females. She's clearly been dead for a few days judging by the damage done by other sea animals." He shook his head. "Damn shame. By the shape of her, we'd thought she was carrying a calf. Looks like she still is. It's a blow to the restoration of the population. We need to determine what killed her. Fisheries and Oceans will want to examine her."

"Well, the body can't stay here. It has to be moved out of the harbor. Now." Sam looked around as if for backing and his gaze seemed to lock on the fisherman she'd been standing beside. "Bert. Get the Zodiac. Back in here and tie a rope to this thing and haul it out to wherever John wants it. It just can't stay here."

"Not going to happen, Sam," John Wilbur said. "Can I have a word in private? Meredith, would you pull yourself together? I need you to call Fisheries and also the police." He dragged Sam aside and they spoke in low, angry voices.

It didn't look like a happy conversation. Sam's voice rose and he looked like he was going to lunge at Wilbur. "What the hell are you playing at, Wilbur?"

John Wilbur shook his head. "I'm not *playing* at anything. But something's not right with this carcass. The tide brought her into town last night, right? And young Alex here was first to spot her." He motioned to the young Aboriginal lad. "Then how come somebody's been able to remove every tooth from her mouth? That's a crime, Sam. Removing and selling the body parts of threatened and endangered species is a crime."

Chapter 2

A CRIME. JOHN WILBUR'S JAW CLENCHED as he faced the other man. The morning seemed to pulse around Phoebe, or maybe it was just the smell getting to her. The wind had ripped up the marine cloud so the sun through the boardwalk was draping bars of light and shadow across the orca body and those around it. The wind whipped the water to small white caps beyond the protection of the harbor and sent long, rolling swells sliding up the stones they stood on. The tide that had left the body there was coming in again.

The little tableau around the whale filled the morning with tension. Sam Rayburn's hands clenched as the woman, Meredith, finally got her emotions under control and fished a phone from her pocket. She dialed and then spoke quietly on the phone, disconnected and dialed again, to speak longer this time.

"Police and Fisheries are on their way," she said. She had a low, whiskey voice that somehow didn't suit her rosy-cheeked face.

"Fine. Have it your way," said Rayburn. "But I don't give a damn who this whale is. When the tide's come in and there's water under that whale, I'm having Bert, here, rope that thing's tail and haul it out of here." Sam turned on his heel, shoved through the crowd, and was gone, back down the gradually flooding beach.

"That's it. Show's over, folks, and there's a hell of a lineup forming at the boat launch," John Wilbur motioned back along the shore. "You heard Sam. He's pissed enough as it is. I'd appreciate it if you didn't piss him off further by holding up the launch line."

The crowd began to disperse, people slip-sliding their way back down the gradually flooding gravel until only the Whale Interpretive Center staff, the Aboriginal boy Alex, and Alice and Phoebe stood there.

"Why would someone take the whale's teeth? That doesn't make sense, does it? May I take a look?" Phoebe asked.

John Wilbur looked down at the whale, the anger he'd shown a moment ago fading into sadness. "Just don't touch her. I don't hold with all the poking and prodding by lookiloos that most of these carcasses have to go through."

Phoebe stiffened. "I'm not a lookiloo. My degree's in biology. I'm just interested in why anyone would want to remove the whale's teeth."

Meredith seemed on the verge of tears again. "She was one of the pod that we see around here all the time. A39. We called her Light Fin, because of the light gray patches on her dorsal fin. I knew it was her as soon as I saw her."

Wilbur shook his head, clearly feeling the loss, too. "As a calf, she befriended a fisherman when she got separated from her pod. Then we helped her find them again, and there was a whole media frenzy about ten years back when we used underwater microphones to lead her back to her family. There is going to be another frenzy when the news gets out." He scrubbed his hands back through his hair.

Phoebe knelt by the animal, studying the whale's head. The eye damage had the uneven shredding of what was probably scavengers—crabs, birds, other fish—the mouth, though…

On the bottom jaw, deep gouges had been made in the flesh by something sharp. Someone had smashed the animal's jaw to loosen the teeth and pulled them out. Alice had shifted over by the Aboriginal lad as Phoebe leaned down for a better look, because the animal's upper gums didn't seem to have the same kind of damage. Odd. The removal method had changed. Instead of hauling the animal's sharp teeth out from the bone, someone had taken a hacksaw to them and had sawed them off at the jaw line.

She glanced up at John Wilbur. Meredith was walking down the beach in the direction of the old cannery. Alice was talking to the Aboriginal boy, Alex.

"Strange, isn't it?" she said. "So why would anyone do this?"

Wilbur shook his head. "How the hell should I know? Why do fishermen shoot them? People are crazy." His voice was bitter.

"It sounds like you've had this sort of thing happen before."

He shook his head. "In Johnstone Strait, the whales are pretty much considered gold. Even the sports fishing charters recognize that they bring in people and money. But we've had our whales disappear when they cycle out of the strait. The cruise ships have been known to kill a few by hitting them. It's one of the reasons people are worried about oil tankers on the coast. Ships that size aren't going to stop for a pod of whales. They can't." He ran his hand back over his head, leaving his hair a little crazed.

"But why take the teeth? Are they valuable?"

"To the whale, sure. To people—well, you can find whale teeth for fifteen dollars at some skeleton dealers. I suppose there are scrimshaw artists who might want them. You can also see them go for a hundred dollars or so on eBay, but those are usually older teeth with some history attached to them. Why go to all this trouble? It makes no sense. Whoever did it probably has no idea it wasn't worth the effort—especially for the cut teeth." He turned to Alex. "Was anyone around when you found her?"

The kid shook his head and looked out to the water.

Perhaps it was John Wilbur's determination to call the carcass "her" instead of "it" and his obvious pain about the whale's loss, but Phoebe found herself liking the man. She stood up and held out her hand. "Phoebe Clay, retired teacher. I used to teach science in Langley Meadows High School."

"John Wilbur. I manage the Whale Interpretive Center." He shook her hand. "Let me guess. You're up here for a whale watching trip."

"Close. A kayaking trip. My niece Alice and I came up early so we could get our sea legs back before we leave for the trip tomorrow. I haven't been kayaking for about five years. I used to do it a lot, though. I always said I'd come to Johnstone Strait to see the whales." And she'd waited to retire to do it.

"Bad luck that the first whale you see is a dead one." Wilbur shook his head.

Worse luck for the whale.

A hail from the boardwalk told them that the police had arrived. A rugged-looking blue-and-white Royal Canadian Mounted Police suburban had parked down the boat launch and a female officer in jeans and a police-issue service jacket started across the gravel to them.

The lad, Alex, looked from the approaching officer to the boardwalk where Meredith had disappeared. Shoulders already hunched in his dark grey hoodie and plaid lumberman's shirt, he shrugged and shifted from foot to foot as if he wanted very badly to leave.

Alice stood beside him, shrugged into her fleece and Gore-Tex.

"John," the officer said as she arrived after her slippery path over the beach.

"Sarah." Wilbur nodded. "This is Phoebe Clay, a biologist. Phoebe, this is Constable Sarah Burns."

Constable Burns was typical of the female constables Phoebe had seen come through the door of her last school. Her thick dark hair was restrained in a tight bun at the back of her head. Her pretty features were laid bare by no makeup as if she was trying hard for a no-nonsense presence. The personal protective vest over the khaki-colored uniform shirt, and the black leather utility belt with weapon, radio, handcuffs, and mysterious leather pouches hid any feminine shape she might have, as if being a woman was a deficit in her line of work. She might be in her early thirties, but already lines of unhappiness had formed around her eyes and drew her mouth downward.

The constable nodded in Phoebe's direction, but the way her attention was on John Wilbur, there was clearly something more than a passing acquaintance between them. The good constable's raised chin and tilt of head, and the attention she paid was similar to that Phoebe had seen in coworkers trying to hide a relationship from colleagues. They stood just a little closer together than an acquaintance normally would, so that the officer had to tilt her head to look up at Wilbur.

"What've we got?" she asked.

"Aside from a dead whale?" Wilbur asked with a tilt of his brow. He stepped to one side. "This isn't just any whale. This is Light Fin. You might remember her from about ten years back."

The constable's eyes widened slightly. "Shit. The young whale who got separated from her pod. This is her?"

Wilbur nodded.

"Well, damn. She just wasn't meant to have a normal life, was she? So why call the police?"

John Wilbur stepped aside so the whale was fully in view. "A couple of things. Because it's her and it's going to be a madhouse here once the news gets out." They both glanced in Phoebe's direction as if she'd be the source of that leak. "And because someone's taken the time to remove all the whale's teeth. In case you weren't aware, it's an offense to tamper with a threatened or endangered species and these whales fit that category."

"You don't need to worry about me or Alice letting that news out," Phoebe said.

Wilbur shrugged. "If I know Sam, he's already on the phone to the media. He's always been one to work the angles—especially if there's the possibility of money coming in. Sarah, Alex was the one who found A39 here early this morning. Sarah, Alex Parker."

All eyes turned on him, and Alex looked like he wanted to bolt. His tall, narrow frame seemed to hunch in on itself as the kid studied his feet. His dark hair hung around his hawk-nosed features.

"What time did you find the whale, Alex?" Constable Burns asked, fishing her notebook out of her breast pocket.

"Uh, I don't know. I don't have a watch. I smelled her and went looking. When I saw what it was, I got the Prof. He told me it was four thirty." He lifted his chin at Wilbur. "Listen, I gotta get home, okay? My parents'll be lookin' for me and my mom worries." He turned to go.

"Hold on there, partner," Constable Burns stopped him. "What did you do when you spotted the carcass?"

"I told you. I called the Prof."

"But you must have come down by the water, right? To make sure of what you were seeing? I mean, you couldn't be sure what you were seeing from up by the buildings. You'd have to come down here to check before waking someone up, right? That's what any normal person would do."

Alex shuffled the stones so they squeaked under him. His hands were rammed into his pockets so his arms were stiff—just like so many of the kids she'd taught, when being grilled about something they didn't want to talk about.

"I came down here, but I didn't do nothin'. She was just like that when I found her." He looked away, out to the dawn-silvered water and the charter fishing boats cruising out of the harbor as if he wanted to escape.

"Did you see anyone around?"

"Here? No I didn't see no one."

The kid looked like he was positively vibrating with the need to run. It could just be that he didn't like the scrutiny—after all, what teenager did—but there was something about him and his answers that said there was more here he just wasn't telling.

"Did you know which whale this was?"

Alex's head shot up and he met the constable's gaze with almost jet-black eyes that held...what? Sorrow? Rage? Fear? Enough that Phoebe wanted to grab Alice away from his side. Then he looked away and he was just a kid, standing in a worn, faded mackinaw shirt and jeans, too early in the morning, who wanted to get home to breakfast or his bed. An odd thought—what teenager got up that early? Or stayed up that late?

"I knew. I seen Light Fin a lot over the years. And the Prof was teaching me about recognizing the whales."

The constable looked back at Wilbur.

"He was helping me with the latest census. Alex is out on the water a lot so he helps identify which whales are around. He's been talking about going to university to study cetaceans. He's already on a scholarship to Prince William Academy."

That was a surprise. It wasn't often you found an Aboriginal youth interested enough in academics to get into that particular school, though that situation was gradually changing. But Alex didn't really fit the academic mold. He acted more like the kids who needed the special education stream with which she was so familiar. That was where the kids with trouble at home, with the law, and in school usually landed. Certainly not at Prince William Academy, one of the most prestigious private schools in the province.

"So you got anymore questions for me?'Cause I really do gotta get going." Alex asked.

Constable Burns lowered her notebook and seemed to consider. "Give me your address and phone number in case I've got anymore questions."

He did, then turned and shuffled off toward the other end of the boardwalk pilings without saying goodbye. There, he slipped into a red kayak and was out and skimming across the water so fast it was like he was a part of it.

"Gotta get home, my ass. That one bears watching," Constable Burns said and looked back at her notebook. She turned to Alice. "And you are?"

Alice's usual youthful exuberance disappeared like a kid being asked to answer a question in class. "Aunt Bee…"

"This is my niece, Alice Standish. We're bystanders. We were heading for our kayaks when we saw the crowd and came down to see what was going on. Whales fascinate me, so we stayed." Phoebe crossed to Alice and put her arm around her niece's shoulders.

"So where were you at around," Constable Burns checked her notes. "At around four thirty this morning?"

"In the campground. Trying to sleep on too-hard ground in a too-thin sleeping bag on a too-cold night with a too-squirmy, almost-teenager at my side."

"Aunt Bee!" Alice elbowed her. "It was not my fault you couldn't sleep."

"Wanna bet?" She tugged a strand of Alice's blonde hair.

"Well, then, thank you for your interest, but I suggest that you head back to your kayaks and let us do our job here."

The good constable couldn't be any clearer. "Okay. Come on, Alice. Professor Wilbur, I hope to see you either out on the water or at the Whale Interpretive Center."

She nodded at Constable Burns and ushered Alice slip-sliding back the way they'd come, pondering what she'd seen. It was bad enough the whale had died. Light Fin had become something of a cultural icon. Heck, she'd even had posters of the whale leaping in her classroom. She'd had her class write papers on what that image meant to them and most of them wrote about her as a symbol of freedom that her students personally yearned for. Rick had.

That someone would deface the animal like that left her all tied up inside.

Chapter 3

IT WAS A GOOD THING THAT THEY LEFT THE whale when they did. The constable had done them a favor kicking them out of the crime scene, because the tide had eaten almost the entire beach so that water was rolling over the tops of the slimy rocks making the footing more treacherous. Overhead the marine cloud had blown away, leaving a vivid blue sky and sunshine that seemed inappropriate, given the tableau back on the rocky shore. When Phoebe glanced over her shoulder, the constable and John Wilbur were crouched beside the whale's head, obviously inspecting the wounds to the mouth.

The wind was brisk as they reached the boat launch, now serving the last of the line of motorboats to be launched. They clambered back up on the concrete only to find the kayaks just about to be rented to some walk-up customers.

It took some smooth talking to get their kayaks back and the box lunches they'd been promised, but then the lad helped them carry the kayaks down to the water. He was a youngster, too—twenty or thereabouts—with bleach-tipped brown hair and a white-toothed grin that looked like it had been tattooed on, because even arguing about the kayaks hadn't wiped it off his face.

"So you take care of all the kayaks, do you?" They were good kayaks—fiberglass—one yellow and one tropical turquoise blue. Both showed the scrape marks of rental kayaks, but the spray skirts and paddles looked like they'd been cared for.

The kid nodded. "I do. All the rentals that come through the resort."

"Is it busy this time of year? I'm surprised you were able to find kayaks for that other couple."

He shrugged. "They'll just have to wait for me to bring 'em down. Won't take but a minute once I get you two out on the water." He helped Alice slide her boat into the cove and then held it steady as she waded in and then settled in the cockpit.

"I'm surprised it's so quiet," Phoebe said.

"It has been the last few summers," he said as he helped Phoebe get her yellow kayak onto the water. "I guess the recession in the US has really hit the number of people coming up here to see the whales. Foreign tourists, too. If they do come, it's just a whale watching trip. And with the news always talking about the failure of the salmon stocks, fishermen think there's nothing here to fish, even though there is. The latest thing is the disappearance of those girls. It's stopped a lot of the family trade." He shook his head. "It keeps on like this, Dad's really going to have to rethink this place."

"Your dad's Sam? The manager?" she asked as she waded to the boat, straddled it, and sank onto the back of the cockpit before sliding her legs and hips inside.

"Nope." He helped her pull the spray skirt down around her cockpit to keep out water and handed her the paddle. "He owns the place. Has these past fifteen years. I'm Trevor, by the way. When you bring the kayaks back today, it'll be Donnie taking care of things. Ask him to call me to come pick them up. Sometimes he forgets."

He gave her kayak a good shove out into the water and waved goodbye.

She dipped her paddle into the water and then paused in a quiet spot to get her rudder foot pedals in the cockpit adjusted to her leg length. When she'd reattached her spray skirt, she found Alice floating beside her.

"You got your rudder set up properly?" Phoebe asked.

"Yup."

"Sunscreen on your face and hands?"

"Yup."

"Something to tie that mop of yours back? Because loose, it's really going to whip your face."

"Aunt Bee..."

"Fine. Have it your way, but don't say I didn't warn you. I haven't had short hair all my life, you know, but make your own mistakes, don't listen to someone older and wiser."

A long-suffering expression on her face, Alice held up her hand to display a wrist with a hair elastic around it. "I got it, okay? If I need it."

Far be it from her aunt to harp on a subject, but when the wind came up hard, about the last thing you had time to think about was fixing your hair. Let the kid find out the hard way. It seemed to be the only way the young ever learned. It had been that way for her, and for every intervening generation that she'd seen. What did that say about human nature?

She dug her paddle into the water and the little boat slipped across the waves of the cove, perfect as you please. Light glittered off the ripples and the paddle spray as she turned the kayak's nose toward the strait and paddled out of the harbor, Alice at her side.

It really was a lovely day, regardless of how it had started. Back on shore, a large blue pickup had arrived and there were two more small figures down along the now-tide-swept shoreline with the carcass. Fisheries and Oceans. She wondered what they would have to say.

"Aunt Bee! Look!" She came back to herself and followed Alice's paddle, pointing out onto the water. A distant group of fins jutted up from the water, the sleek black backs dolphining through the waves. "Oh my God, oh my God, oh my God!"

"Maybe we can catch up to them. Come on!" Phoebe propelled the kayak forward, skimming through the waves. Around them spread the grandeur of Johnstone Strait. It ran northwest to southeast along the northeastern edge of Vancouver Island, bounded to the east by the Broughton Archipelago that filled the space between Vancouver Island and the mainland coast. This area of the Inland Passage had a rich ecology, including many species of animal.

But most of all there were the whales. The great dark fins cut through the glistening water, back-dropped by the misty green of the archipelago islands about three and a half miles distant and the ragged white peaks of the coastal mountain range beyond. At a distance, a red kayak flew like a bug across water. Alex, most probably, going to be with live whales after being with the dead. Farther out on the water, a few sport fishing boats were pulling up their lines and aiming for the whales—it seemed everyone wanted to see them.

Phoebe dug in her paddle and checked over her shoulder. Alice was giving it all she had, but the girl wasn't as powerful as Phoebe was. She lagged behind, her gaze locked on the whales that were getting too far ahead. The darn blackfish were getting away.

Phoebe slowed her paddle and Alice came up alongside. Her jaw was set, her eyes narrowed against the sunlight, her cheeks bright with exertion.

"I don't think we're going to catch them, sweetie," Phoebe tried.

"No. We're going to. We just have to keep paddling." Alice wouldn't even look at her and her eyes were shining too brightly—as if she was close to crying.

"Honey, there'll be other days when we're out for the five-day camping trip, and maybe even more today. There's supposedly over a hundred and fifty orcas in Johnstone Strait. That means our chances are pretty good. So don't go exhausting yourself today."

Alice gave her the unhappy glare. "*You* don't know that. You have no idea whether I'm exhausted or not." She shook her head as the whales disappeared down the coastline beyond them, then thunked her paddle down on the top of the kayak. "So if we're not seeing whales, what else is there?"

"We-ll," Phoebe knew she had to tread carefully here. She and Alice had always had a great relationship. It was what had made it seem like such a great idea for her to take her niece who was—according to Becca—growing testier every day, and give Phoebe's long-suffering sister a break.

"We could race for the shore because I understand that there could be otters around and maybe even a beach to have lunch," Phoebe said. "Or I could dump your kayak and see if all those re-entering-your-kayak exercises we did at home really meant something. Your choice."

She rested her own paddle on her kayak and made a show of enjoying the scenery. It wasn't exactly a show. The place was world-class gorgeous with the tall trees coming down to the rocky cliffs along the water, the surf lightly crashing, and even an eagle floating on thermals overhead.

"Look!" she pointed at the bird. "He's struggling. It looks like he's got a big fish or something."

Alice shaded her eyes. "You're right! One big fish." When she looked back she was smiling again. "Sorry I got upset. I just really want to see whales."

"Gee, ya think? But we will. Today, though, is all about getting our paddling worked out so that tomorrow those whales won't stand a chance."

She got a nod from Alice and then the rotten kid sent her kayak surging forward. "Last one to the shore has to roll their boat!"

No way in heck was she going to be stuck doing that. She'd thought she was going to drown the last time. Upper body strength was not exactly her forte.

She sent her kayak after Alice, listening to the girl's shrieks of laughter as she realized her aunt was catching up. Their kayaks surged toward the rocky cliffs, but there was no place to land so they angled southeast and headed down the coast side-by-side. Both of them settled into a nice comfortable rhythm that worked the upper back and not the shoulders. The day around them was a blue-green dream of warm sun, light breeze, blue ocean and sky.

As the sun rose higher, they rounded a headland and found a secluded little cove with a strip of white beach backed by forest. The two of them coasted into shore together in silent agreement, their race long forgotten.

The fiberglass hulls of the kayaks shushed against the sand as Phoebe pulled her spray skirt loose and shoved herself up out of the cockpit. Alice did the same, but a darn sight quicker, and stepped onto shore. "You lose. You have to tip your kayak," said in a triumphant sing-song voice.

"But-but-but... I thought we weren't racing anymore!" Phoebe said in mock indignation and splashed into shore.

"You might not have been, but I still was." Alice's big baby blues shone up at her. Then she grinned and gave a long-suffering sigh. "All right. I guess I can let you off this time."

"You better. I've got the food." Phoebe beached her kayak next to flotsam that included a bit of marine rope and a cast-off sneaker—by its size, likely some kid's off one of the fishing or whale watching boats. She gave Alice a hand drawing her kayak up the beach. Then Phoebe made camp in the middle of the sun-warmed sand beside the kayaks. She spread a blanket that had been stowed in her boat while Alice explored along the shoreline.

It was so quiet. The sound of the waves shuffling along the shoreline, of Alice's footsteps in the sand as she picked up stones along the water. The distant drone of a boat engine on the strait and the sound of an eagle's cry, though she could not spot the bird.

Seated on the blanket, she leaned back on her braced arms and raised her face to the sun. This was why she'd come here—for a quiet place to get her thoughts back in order after the crash and burn at work. If she could just have time like this to decompress, then maybe she could go back to work again and not "retire" as the school board and her doctor had asked her to do. She was still a young woman, relatively speaking. It was just the pressure of the job that had got to her.

A shadow blocking her sun brought her eyes open. Alice, looking windblown but happy.

"You ready for lunch?" Phoebe asked.

"Famished. Sorry, but your scrambled eggs didn't really fill me up this morning."

"Growing girl." Phoebe sat cross-legged to leave room for Alice and pulled their lunch bags open. Two bottles of water. Two multigrain bagels with cream cheese and something that looked like tuna and alfalfa sprouts. An apple and an orange so they would need to arm wrestle for the apple. Last were two gigantic oatmeal cookies chock full of raisins.

Alice set a palm-full of pretty stones she'd collected on the top of her kayak and then folded down onto the sun-warmed blanket.

"Did you find anything interesting?"

Alice shrugged as she bit into her bagel after examining its contents with a curled-lip frown. "I don't like cream cheese, but this is pretty good." She munched thoughtfully. "That was really bad this morning, wasn't it? The whale, I mean."

Phoebe nodded. "Pretty sad. Light Fin. I remember using her as a jumping-off place to get my students thinking about the environment. She was like an ambassador to the wild."

"I wrote about her when I was in grade three. They made us watch an old video about her and write an essay. The video said she was a dead ancestor come to bring Aboriginal people a message. For my essay I wrote about what that message was—to save her people, the whales. I did a whole bunch of research about how endangered all the whales are. It was scary to think of a world with no whales in it. Especially when you listen to their music."

Phoebe took a bite of her sandwich and pulled Alice into her side. "Sometimes you make me really proud, you know."

They leaned back against the blue kayak side-by-side and let the wind play with their hair as they finished their sandwiches. They decided to save the fruit and cookies for later.

"I think I'm just going to lie here for a while and catch a bit of a nap," Phoebe said. And think about Light Fin. How had she died? Who would scavenge her teeth?

"'Kay. I'm just going to explore the beach."

"Just don't go too far and remember that there could be bears coming down to the shore. You stay by the water. If you hear anything in the woods, you hightail it back here. Okay?"

Alice nodded and stood, heading back to explore along the receding shoreline. The tide, which had come in after Light Fin had been found, had started to recede again in the few hours they'd been paddling. It had receded farther since they'd beached, revealing an area of round pebbles and larger, seaweed-covered rocks that would provide lots of nooks and crannies to explore.

Her niece was crouched by a tidal pool as Phoebe lay back and closed her eyes. After the few hours' sleep last night, a nap would be heaven. Her mind wandered over the black-and-white body on the stones of the harbor. She fell asleep wondering just what or who would do that to an orca.

Dark night. Dark waves. Dark whale. She was alone, cutting through the water in search of her pod, powerful tail sending her forward like a torpedo, breath coming in powerful bursts from her blowhole. She had to go faster because something was coming. Something was after her, big and dark and powerful that stole the stars from the sky, blocked the light of the moon. It shook her world around her and stole all the breath from her lungs. A blow and she was dying, fighting to stay afloat, to live, to protect her unborn calf.

"Aunt Bee? Are you all right?"

The voice brought her, gasping, up from a dark place where her voice was drowned and she felt so helpless she could scream. Her eyes opened on blue and for a moment she couldn't remember where she was. Wind in her hair. Sun on her face. *She should be in the principal's office, convincing him he was wrong. They had to do something instead of sitting in her office.*

"Aunty Bee?" The worry in the voice brought her up to sitting and she blinked to steady herself. Not an office. A beach. And she was—her eyes flickered from her niece, who should be three thousand miles away with her mother, and then locked on the kayaks beside her. Kayaking with Alice. Right. She scrubbed her face.

"My goodness, that was a nightmare. I dreamed I was Light Fin and something killed me."

Alice was looking at her with concern in her eyes. She held something in her palm, but she closed her hand and shoved it in her pocket. "You—you're okay now, though, right?"

Was she? She felt shaky as heck and weaker than she'd felt since... well... since she'd gone off work. "I'm fine." She pushed up to her feet, but had to lean on her yellow kayak to steady herself while she checked her watch. "Two o'clock! You shouldn't have let me sleep so long!"

"You looked like you needed it. And you were so peaceful—until the last bit. I—I tried to wake you, so I grabbed your shoulders and shook. You still didn't wake. I—I slapped you. I'm sorry."

The look of concern had melted to reveal an underlay of visceral fear. The poor kid was on a beach three thousand miles from home and the only adult she knew had gone wonky. No wonder she was afraid.

"I'm sorry, Ali. Really sorry. I don't know what happened. I must have been more tired than I realized." But she'd had vivid visceral dreams like this before, hadn't she? She shook her head trying to rid herself of the haunted feeling. This wasn't the same. This was a whale, for God's sake. She stood fully upright and grinned. "Up for more paddling?"

"Are you sure? Maybe you need more rest," Alice said, far too old for her age—the problem with being an only child.

"I'm a-okay to get paddling. It'll get the blood circulating and maybe we'll see more whales."

With the tide ebbing, the beach had gotten considerably larger since they'd beached. They had to haul the kayaks down the sand and over pebbles and then slip and slide over a rough bench of slimy stone and barnacles before they reached enough water to set the kayaks down. Both of them were puffing by the time the two kayaks were shifted and they'd donned their spray skirts and settled in their cockpits again.

'You all right, Aunty Bee?"

"Just fine, honey. Now quit being concerned. I just needed to wake up is all, and believe me, I'm awake now." She pulled on her sunglasses and noted that Alice had tamed her hair into a ponytail. "How about we go a little farther down the shore and then we can head back to Pirate Cove, get cleaned up, and have dinner in one of their restaurants?"

Alice nodded from her spot floating closer to the mouth of the cove.

"Good. Last one to that rock at the entrance to the cove is a rotten egg." Phoebe dug her paddle into the water and sent her yellow kayak surging forward trying to pass Alice.

Alice yelped and scrambled her paddle into the waves, raising a heck of a spray of water. Then she caught her rhythm and darned if she didn't set a heck of a pace. Phoebe shouted and paddled harder, the effort shredding the last of the haunting. She was on vacation, for God's sake. She was with her niece, going to paddle with whales. She couldn't get much farther from her work than that.

But darned if Alice didn't hold her own. The kid really threw everything she had at it and Phoebe was straining to make up the head start she'd given her. They were neck-in-neck when they coasted past the rock at the cove entrance and out into Johnstone Strait proper.

Phoebe hooted. Alice shouted to the sky. Then together they turned southward, their paddles flashing in unison in the sunlight.

"Thank you for letting me come with you." Alice broke the silence of wind and water.

"Thank you for coming with me. It wouldn't have been near as much fun without you—even if you are a squirmy bedmate." She nodded at Alice because it was true. It would have been a lonely night and day on her own. She realized that now.

They paddled another twenty minutes south, passing patches of beach and even catching a glimpse of what they thought was a bear feeding amongst the low bushes on a bluff. But then the bear disappeared into the trees and Phoebe checked her watch. "I think we'd better head back if we want that dinner; and if possible, I'd like to check out the Whale Interpretive Center."

It was a long paddle home, much farther than they'd realized. To their advantage, the tide turned and the wind died down and that helped them paddle north, past the cove where they'd had lunch and the cliff-lined shore. They saw the eagle again, or another one, they couldn't say for sure, and finally reached the narrow entrance to Pirate Cove.

The cove was in shadow, the sun sinking toward the west, limning the resort's multi-colored buildings with light, but leaving their faces in shadow. The charter fishing boats were all chugging into harbor, a few of them showing off fish they had caught.

They drove their kayaks in to the side of the boat launch that was busy with the boats returning from a day of fishing. Phoebe took care of signing the kayaks back in and reintroduced herself to Bert Clarke's son, Donnie. She retrieved their leftover fruit and cookies that they'd never eaten and found Alice waiting for her, staring out at the town and the harbor.

"It's not there," she said. "Light Fin's gone."

She was right. The carcass no longer rested under the boardwalk. "They must have done what that man, Sam, wanted, and towed her back out to sea again. Or taken her someplace else to examine."

"Aunt Bee?" The girl gave her a worried look.

"What is it, honey?" That look said maybe the child saw how the dream and the whale on the beach had preoccupied her on the paddle back. Damn, she had to get her head on straight or something bad would happen.

"Don't be mad, okay?"

"Mad about what?"

Alice held out her hand and opened it. On it lay a large, off-white curved stone. "I found it while you were sleeping."

Not a stone.

A tooth.

One end had been sawed smooth.

Chapter 4

So much for a shower and nice dinner. Still feeling windblown and briny with her face and hair caked in salt from the wind, Phoebe led Alice toward the low red building at the boardwalk's far end. The light was fading as the sun fell behind the Vancouver Island mountains, plunging Pirate Cove into the grey light of pre-twilight. The wind off the water seemed to carry a chill and their footsteps on the boardwalk rumbled like thunder.

"Alice, come on."

"I'm coming, all right. I don't see what all the fuss is about."

Phoebe stopped dead in her tracks. "You don't see. Think about it. That whale had all of its teeth either smashed out of its jaw or cut off at the jaw line. You found one of the teeth in that cove. Does that suggest anything?"

Alice considered a moment—just like a kid put on the spot in school. "Maybe the whale was originally there—in the cove?"

Phoebe touched her nose. "Bingo."

One pair of blue eyes grew huge and round. "You mean we could have been eating where the dead whale was?"

"Well that's pretty unlikely given how far up the beach we were, but the whale might have been wherever you found the tooth. When the tide came in, it might have picked the body up and carried it back out into the sound. Then the waves pushed it in here where it was found."

"You got all that just from one tooth?"

Phoebe put her arm around Alice and ushered her toward the Whale Interpretive Center. "Let's just say it's a reasonable deduction."

The Interpretive Center looked like it was locked up tight, the 'open' sign turned off. Phoebe still tried the door. The knob turned in her hand and she pushed inside, a little ship's bell recording announcing their entry. Shadows filled the single large room, with the other end of the building lost in gloom. Strung along the walls and suspended from the high, two-story ceiling were bones. Large bones that made skeletons of various sizes, the largest of which filled a large, roped-off area that took up most of the center of the room.

"Whoa," Alice inhaled and stepped past Phoebe. "Look at the size of that thing." She went up to the central skeleton and reached out to touch the yellowed bone. "Fin whale," she read off the display card. "What did they do, hunt it down and then take the skeleton?"

"Professor Wilbur?" Phoebe called, uneasily closing the door behind her. The room was close and had a strange odor of salt and dust, but there seemed to be air moving from vents up above.

There was no answer, but a thump came from the dark end of the building.

"Is there anyone here?" It was possible that Pirate Cove was such a small town that they just left their buildings unlocked and open. No way. Not with valuable skeletons like these. Probably someone was just in back finishing up before locking the doors for the day. She led Alice down along the length of the arched rib bones of the fin whale, past similar yellowing bones of a porpoise, a bear, a seal, and other skulls and paraphernalia that might have excited even the jaded tastes of her alternate school students. Like a kid in a dinosaur park, Alice positively dragged behind her she was so busy taking everything in.

Another thump from ahead in the darkness and Phoebe slowed. They must be at the other end of the building; she could just make out the wall and a door. "Hello?"

There was still no answer. Another thump and she motioned Alice behind her, suddenly feeling vulnerable and foolish for leading her niece into a building she had no right to be in. She went up to the door and knocked again. Another thump and something crashed to the floor. Run for help, or open the door?

She looked back at Alice and motioned her back, then tried the knob on the door. Just like the front door, it turned.

Okay, Phoebe Clay, time to make a decision. You going to take a chance on finding something you don't want to when you are supposed to be taking care of a twelve-year-old? You pushed your nose in where it wasn't wanted before and look where it got you.

She swallowed. She'd never veered away before when something was wrong, and she wasn't going to do so now, because something was wrong in Pirate Cove, even if it just involved a whale. She pushed the door open.

A rasping cry and a scream, and then large wings battered her head, talons slashed at her face, and then whatever-it-was was gone, up to the darkness of the main room's ceiling amidst the chains that suspending the fin whale skeleton. The huge bones swayed, creaking, while from overhead came the sound of wings battering against the boards. There was a crash and a square piece of something came smashing to the ground, almost hitting

Phoebe's head. She threw herself against the wall and stood there trembling, her heart pumping like mad.

"Aunt Bee! Aunt Bee! Are you all right?" Warm arms came around her and held on tight. Phoebe held on for dear life in return.

She took a deep breath. "What the heck was that? It was huge."

"It looked like an eagle, except it was black instead of having a white head."

Eagle? What the heck was an eagle doing in the back room of the Whale Interpretive Center?

She set Alice away and went back to the door. It had partially closed after the bird had flown. Through the remaining opening there was only darkness. She went to push the door open a second time.

"Who's there?" demanded a female voice from back near the door. She almost leapt out of her skin. Alice huddled up to her, peering over Phoebe's shoulder.

Her heart thud-thud-thudding so fast it felt like thunder, Phoebe swallowed again.

"We are. We were looking for Professor Wilbur." Phoebe ran her hands back through her tangled hair and grabbed Alice's hand. Together they started back down along the whale skeleton as banks of lights suddenly flashed on to spotlight all the gleaming bones. At the entrance stood the woman from this morning. What was her name?

The dark-haired woman looked her coolly up and down. She was in her thirties, Mediterranean with olive skin and long hair that fell down to her shoulders. She still wore the blue Whale Interpretive Center jacket she'd worn that morning along with jeans and a pair of gumboots. "I'm Ayisha Meredith, John Wilbur's assistant. What do you need him for?"

"We might have information about the dead whale in the harbor this morning." Phoebe was surprised at the calmness of her voice even though her heart was still pounding—the product of years of holding it together in front of a class. "Where can we find him?"

"John? He's not here now. They pulled the whale out to a cove north of town during high tide. They'd doing a necropsy there."

Phoebe took that in and felt herself swaying. Sighed. At least they still had the apples and the cookies, but she really should get Alice something to eat. "I guess we'll need directions."

"Directions?"

"To the cove."

The woman put her hands to her hips. "I'm not giving out that information to a couple of lookiloos. If you've got something to tell John, you can tell me and I'll get him the information."

The woman acted like some politician's assistant trying to keep her politico out of the line of fire, but darn it, she needed to see the professor or… "You can tell me where he is, or I can go to the police with the information. Your choice."

The Meredith woman's gaze narrowed and she looked like she could swear. Phoebe pulled Alice to her and shoved past the woman to head for the door. If she wasn't getting the information she needed, she could at least get them both dinner. "We're staying at the campground, site sixty-three, if he's interested. We'll phone the police from the restaurant. Oh, and if you had an eagle in the back storeroom, it's gotten loose and is somewhere up there. Sorry about that." She waved her hand at the ceiling, smiled sweetly, and hauled Alice out the door.

"What was that all about?" Alice looked up at her, her face pale in the fading twilight.

"Darned if I know. A strange reaction when we're just offering to help."

Still crusty with brine from their paddle—salt air got into everything and stuck, she'd forgotten that about it—they got a seat in the coffee-shop-cum-restaurant that sat up on the boardwalk and ordered a meal. This late in the day there were very few patrons in the little restaurant. When they'd pushed the door open, one husband and wife couple was just leaving and a couple of fishermen types were just finishing their meal. She recognized Bert from the waterfront and nodded. He nodded back.

The restaurant itself was a plain little place, as if it was a no-nonsense answer to a hungry fisherman's prayers. The walls were white, the floor fake wood. The tables simply set with plain flatware and paper placemats with the kitschy little Pirate Cove logo of a pirate riding a whale. The waitress, a mousy little brunette with a ponytail and *"Trish"* stenciled on the pocket of her pale yellow polo shirt, brought them water glasses without so much as a smile so that Phoebe wasn't holding her breath about the quality of the food. The only hope was that the place smelled, well, good.

Heavenly, in fact, with the scent of grilled meat and fish, a hint of spice and fresh herbs, but that could just be the fact that her stomach felt like her throat had been cut.

Phoebe ordered local deep fried oysters, a specialty of northern Vancouver Island, while Alice curled her lip at seafood and ordered a burger with fries. And a strawberry milkshake. And double chocolate cake for dessert.

The kid still had a hollow leg, while Phoebe would gain weight just sitting this close to all those calories.

While they waited for their food, Phoebe pulled out her cell phone. She'd kept it in a small Ziploc bag in case she'd gotten dumped in the water, and did a search for the non-emergency police phone number in Pirate Cove. Hit dial and hauled the phone to her ear. It buzzed, buzzed again and then clicked as if it was going through relays.

"Port Hardy RCMP, how may I direct your call?"

"I'm trying to get in touch with the constable who dealt with a call about a dead whale in Pirate Cove this morning," she said.

"May I ask what this is about?" the operator said.

"I believe I have some new evidence, but I need to talk to her tonight. We leave on a kayaking trip tomorrow morning at six a.m."

Alice groaned across the table and Phoebe grinned at her. The way she was feeling, she could totally relate. They should already be in bed—she just hoped they could sleep tonight.

"Can I have your name, please?"

She gave it and made sure they had her telephone number and their spot in the campground. She also advised that they were in the restaurant in case the police officer could come now. She hung up just as the food arrived. The waitress dropped their plates on the table and then, as if to make a point, turned the "open" sign off by the door. Okay, so they'd just made it in under the wire, but the girl didn't have to make her resentment so obvious. At least not if she wanted a reasonable tip.

The food was far better than Phoebe'd predicted. The oysters were tender and breaded and deep fried to perfection so they crunched perfectly in her mouth—a combination of briny oyster and a hint of spice that might be coriander. Accompanying them was a homemade tartar sauce, a side of perfectly crisp fries, and a small side salad with a delicate raspberry vinaigrette that she wolfed down. Surprisingly, they had chai milk tea on the menu and she sipped that with her meal, reveling in the wonderful mix of cardamom, cinnamon, and pepper that made her think of the comfort of rolling into bed and tugging up the covers.

The two fishermen left and that left Phoebe and Alice alone in the restaurant. The girl was tucking into her food like she hadn't eaten in a week. Phoebe grinned across at her as she dipped an excellent crispy fry into a little tub of ketchup on her plate. "Good, huh?"

"This is the best burger ever. Don't tell Mom I said so."

Phoebe zipped her lips. "You've got that thing you found today someplace safe?"

The girl patted her chest. "Inside pocket."

"How about you give it to me and I'll keep it safe in the baggy with my phone?"

Alice shrugged and kept eating while she fished for the tooth in her jacket pocket and handed it over, just as Phoebe's phone rang. She slipped the tooth into the bag and the bag into her pocket as she answered the phone.

"Ms. Clay? Constable Sarah Burns returning your call. I was told you might have information pertinent to the investigation into that whale this morning."

"Actually, yes." The restaurant was empty except for the waitress, but for some reason she didn't like the idea of anyone overhearing what she had to say. "My niece and I—we met you this morning at the whale. Well, we went out paddling this morning and I believe we found something—or my niece did—that might be pertinent to your investigation. Is there any way you could come to Pirate Cove so that I can give it to you?"

There was silence at the end of the line for so long that for a moment Phoebe thought they'd been cut off. Then: "What have you found, Ms. Clay?"

"I'd rather not say, given I'm in a public place, but we may have stumbled upon where the whale was—damaged."

The waitress pushed a mop and bucket out of the kitchen. Through the open door Phoebe caught a glimpse of the cook and two other figures. One, dressed in white, was the young man Alex, from the harbor this morning. Small world—smaller village. The other had his back to her but had longish, salt-stained brown hair just over his collar. They were deep in discussion, but before the door swung shut again, Alex met her gaze and quickly looked away.

A sigh came across the phone lines. "All right. But it's going to take me about twenty minutes to get there. I'm out at the whale necropsy right now."

"I'll see you at our campsite in about twenty minutes, then. Perhaps you can advise Professor Wilbur of my call. I went looking for him when we came back from our trip, but ended up only speaking to his assistant, Ms. Meredith. She said she'd get the information to him."

The waitress had started mopping as Phoebe hung up. Alice was finishing her meal, slurping the last of her milkshake up through a straw, the cake she'd ordered now nothing more than chocolate crumbs and smeared icing on a plate.

Wondering what kind of person could shatter a whale's jaw to get at the teeth, or hacksaw them off, Phoebe drained the last of the chai tea down and slipped her phone back in the plastic bag and back in her pocket. Then she paid the bill, left a fifteen percent tip for the quality of the food when she should have left nothing for the unfriendly service, and they pushed outside into darkness.

The air had gone still in the night, allowing mist to rise off the water and coalesce around the eerie halogen lights of the village and harbor. The white buildings were stained amber, the red Interpretive Center gone umber and dark. From the harbor came the tink-tink-tink of the faint breeze jangling the marine hardware on the few sailboats at harbor and the slurp and gurgle of water around wooden pilings as if the ocean was gradually drinking them all down. She shivered and peered out into the darkness of the sky. No stars were visible because of the thick mist overhead, and for a moment déjà vu swept through her and she felt lost and alone except for Alice, who she had to protect at all costs. Her heart hitched in her chest, but she shook it off.

"Come on, kiddo, let's go get you that shower and get you to bed." She inhaled the seawater and seaweed scents laced with cedar and followed the boardwalk to the boat ramp before turning uphill toward the campground.

It was dark, as if the night was immersed in velvet—the darkness like a threatening caress on her cheeks. Once the road curved up and around away from the village proper, there were no lights, just the darkness, the potholed road, and the potholes to stumble in. The sound of the ocean became background noise, but otherwise there wasn't even the sound of a car engine.

"I've never seen it so dark," Alice said. With the moon dark tonight, she was a half-seen ghost beside Phoebe.

"This is what night's really like—what humans lived with for millennia until they made fire and then invented electric lights. Think about it, Alice. It wasn't that many centuries ago that people huddled around a fire because they couldn't stand the darkness. And there are places in the world where they still depend on fire to banish the night. Africa. Places in the mountains and in the north and far south. Where we live in North America, we rarely see the true night because of light pollution." She stopped and pointed to the sky. "Look."

Overhead, the ocean mists parted like filmy curtains exposing the mass of the Milky Way galaxy spreading its arms. "Imagine what's out there, Alice. Imagine what it must have been like to live in the darkness and have that staring down at you every night. That's where the story of heaven comes from—the wonder of staring at the sky."

Alice said nothing, but she stood there, staring upward at the wedge of the sky between the tall trees. When she finally looked back at Phoebe, it was like she'd captured the starlight in her eyes. Together they walked up the gravel road to where the low lights of the RVs and the bright beam of the light over the shower house pushed back the night again. Phoebe hauled their sleeping bags and Therm-a-Rests out of her car and Alice scooted off to the washroom for a shower and to do her teeth while Phoebe set up the tent interior for sleeping. At least keeping their bedding in the car had stopped it from getting damp. She even started the car for a few minutes and lay the sleeping bags over the heat vents to warm them a little.

The big white-and-blue suburban rolled into the campground just as Alice returned and was getting settled in the tent. The kid looked like she'd sleep like the dead. Phoebe hoped.

Phoebe stood up from where she'd been fussing in her car to meet the constable.

Sarah Burns stepped out of her car looking every bit as officious as this morning and a mite more impatient. "Ms. Clay?"

Phoebe stuck out her hand. "Thank you for coming. You must have had a long day."

The woman managed a small, rueful smile. In the light of her vehicle and the flickering shower house light, her dark hair was no longer quite as neat as it had been. A dark streak ran down her cheek as if she'd handled something and inadvertently marked herself.

"A little bit," she said. "And it doesn't look like it's going to end anytime soon. What have you got for me, Ms. Clay?"

Phoebe hauled out her phone and emptied the tooth out into her hand.

"This. Alice, my niece, and I were out paddling today to get our sea-legs before our kayak trip tomorrow. At lunch we stopped at a little cove just south of here—it must be the first one after you pass all the cliffs along the way. Anyway, we stopped and had lunch and I had a nap while Alice explored the tidal pools. She found it there, but didn't tell me she'd found it until we were back here. Given it looked like it had been sawed off, I immediately thought of Light Fin and how someone had messed with her carcass."

Constable Clay had her flashlight out and examined the tooth. "It could be from another whale."

"It could."

"But you don't think so." Constable Clay met Phoebe's gaze.

"No. I don't. Alice showed me generally where she'd found the tooth. It was quite a ways out from the beach, but it looked like a place where the carcass might have beached and could have been found when the tide was out. Whoever it was could have removed the teeth and then the tide could have come in and wave action could have washed the carcass back out to the water and into Pirate Cove."

At least the constable placed the tooth in an evidence bag and had her notebook out. She asked more questions about the small cove and the general location where Alice had found the tooth. When she was done, she flipped her notebook closed.

"I'd like to interview your niece."

Phoebe shook her head. "I'm afraid that's not possible right now. The girl's exhausted and she's already asleep. Tomorrow we're supposed to meet with the kayak tour operator at six a.m. If you can be at the boat launch around then, I suppose you can talk to her, but I warn you that mornings are not her best time. She's twelve, you know?"

Constable Burns apparently had no concept, for she said she'd see them in the morning and left. Phoebe stood there in the darkness and watched the taillights of the police vehicle disappear out of the campground. She looked up at the sky and breathed in deeply, seeking calm.

For some strange reason, it didn't come.

Chapter 5

THE NIGHT WAS A NIGHTMARE AND the morning was worse. Phoebe went for her shower to sluice off the worst of the salt and sea spray—except the hot water turned off half way through her shower so by the time she was finished she was ice cold and shivering as she ran back to the tent. Alice was still dead to the world, which was good, but as frequently happens with the young, she had her legs and arms spread out and crowded Phoebe so she seemed to be lying on a huge knot of root. With that in her back, she never did get to sleep, just lay there listening to Alice's gentle breathing, the steady background roar of the ocean, and her own heart beating. Sometime in the middle of the night she must have dozed, because when she woke up it was raining—hard—and she hadn't put a tarp up over the tent because there had been no rain in the forecast.

Perfect.

The beep of her phone alarm at four thirty a.m. was not what she wanted to hear, but she groaned and rolled over, almost ready to forego the kayaking trip for a few more minutes in the warmth of her sleeping bag. Instead she sat up and gave Alice a little shake, succeeding only in provoking a low groan and hiss that sounded suspiciously like a snake. And the little jewel was only twelve. God help her mother when she hit thirteen, the witching age.

She hauled on her bra under her sleeping shirt and then pulled on a t-shirt and fleece and Gore-Tex jacket. A pair of Lycra shorts and her athletic sandals and she was good to go. She climbed out of the tent. Still dark, but dawn was threatening and, while the rain had stopped, it seemed to have gathered in a thick cloud that rested on the treetops.

"Come on, Alice. You want to see whales, you've got to get up. I'm going to run to the showers and then I'll be back to cook up a little breakfast. I'd like you up and dressed when I get back."

Trust. Trust was the answer with kids so she was just going to trust that Alice's desire to see the whales was more than enough to get her out of bed—no matter how tired she might be.

Phoebe trudged over to the showers and washed her face. The bags under her brown eyes, if anything, looked worse. Like she could pack an entire wardrobe in them. Her short blonde hair was a halo of spikes. She tried flattening it by palming water onto her head and finally turned on a shower—still flipping cold—and stuck her head in.

Bad words escaped her, but she could make her hair behave and she was surely to God awake now. She trudged back to the car and hauled out the camp stove, set it up, and started a pot of coffee. From inside the tent came the sound of stirring and then the zipper unzipped and a grinning Alice stuck her head out. "I've got the sleeping bags and Therm-a-Rests rolled."

"Good girl. Now skedaddle over to the washroom and I'll put some oatmeal on."

Alice screwed up her face but jogged across to the showers. Phoebe filled a pot with bottled water and added oats, then set it on the burner, stirring. Some maple sugar and fresh blueberries and two bowls and there was breakfast ready just as Alice came back, her cheeks pink in the cool morning. They ate together perched on the sodden picnic table bench and then Alice took the pot and bowls off to the shower house to wash while Phoebe started taking down the tent. Tonight they'd be camping somewhere out on the five-day kayak trip.

Taking down the tent was not fun at the best of times. Really not fun with the nylon soaking wet. She hauled the rolled-up sleeping bags and pads from the tent and then removed the metal dome supports outside. The sodden canvas sagged in on itself. So not nice wrestling it into a semblance of order, pulling out stakes and then folding the canvass up for rolling. The only good thing was that she had set the tent up on a tarp so the bottom wasn't filthy. When Alice came back, it took both of them to stuff the darn tent in its bag, load the car, and drive down to the boat launch. It was five forty-five and a blue-and-white police suburban waited.

There were also nine kayaks—including two doubles—a guide, and eight excited people—ten when they arrived. Phoebe parked and she and Alice lugged their bags down to the kayaks. The door of the police suburban opened as they passed and Constable Burns stepped out.

"Ms. Clay? Is this your niece that I need to talk to?"

Alice shot her an uncertain glance. "Aunt Bee?"

Phoebe sighed. "Hold on a moment, Constable. Let us get our things settled. Alice, you were asleep by the time Constable Burns arrived. She needs to ask you a few questions about where you found the tooth, all right?"

Constable Burns trailed after them as Phoebe went to the guide, who was inspecting the kayaks. "Morning. I'm Phoebe Clay. This is my niece, Alice."

"Mike Hrycon. Welcome." He shook both their hands. "You can stash your stuff there for the briefing." He was a youngish man, most likely in his thirties, with shaggy brown hair down to his shoulders and a thin, whiplash build that was all sinew and muscle. He wore a wetsuit over his legs, the top left to fold back around his hips from the waist.

"Pleased to meet you, Mike. Listen, the police need to talk to us. We'll just be a few minutes. I hope that's okay."

She didn't wait for an answer as he checked his watch—couldn't, with Constable Burns breathing down her neck, so she turned Alice back to the waiting constable. "We're here. Sorry. This is going to have to be quick."

Constable Burns pulled out her notebook. "Alice, what's your full name?"

"Alice. Alice Clay-Standish."

Burns wrote it down.

"How old are you?"

Alice glanced in Phoebe's direction. She nodded.

"I'm twelve."

"Twelve, huh. What grade does that put you in?"

"I'm going into grade eight."

"So how was grade seven?"

Alice rolled her eyes. "It was fine. Great. Last year in elementary school, what do you think? A bore."

Yup, there came the attitude. "Alice, just answer the questions, hon."

"I am, okay?" She kept looking at the kayaks and the other kayakers, half with mortification and half with longing. The others were donning spray skirts, laughing at the sagging skirts of neoprene they now all wore—and casting uncomfortable glances in their direction.

"Your aunt tells me that you found something yesterday. A tooth. Can you tell me about that?"

Constable Burns finally had Alice's attention.

"Well, we were out kayaking and we decided to race into a cove we saw and have lunch. I won the race and we beached the kayaks and ate. Then Aunt Bee had a nap—I guess I kept her awake the night before—and I explored the beach. The tide was out, so I was exploring the tidal pools. At least they were pretty clean. I couldn't believe the junk on the beach—there was even someone's perfectly good sweater just left. Anyway, I was looking at the tidal pools and one of them had this weird deposit of white dust in it, so I was looking at it and there was the tooth in the sand. I picked it up and was going to ask my Aunt about it at the beach, but...things...happened and I forgot."

"What kind of things?"

Alice cast a glance in Phoebe's direction. "My aunt woke up like she'd had a bad dream. It kinda scared me, so I didn't remember to show her the tooth until we got back to the harbor. Then we tried to take it to the Whale Interpretive Center and then we called you." She shrugged.

The guide was looking at them and checking his watch. He wanted to get on with his orientation and the other kayakers were starting to give them strange looks. It wasn't going to help them fit in on the trip at all.

"Where was this tidal pool, Alice? We need to know because we want to search the cove today."

"Wellll." The girl thought a moment. "I think it was pretty much in the middle of the cove, 'cause we beached the kayaks in the center and it wasn't that far from them. I think it might have been fifteen to twenty feet down from the beach on the rocks. It wasn't that far before the stone dropped off into deeper water. Only maybe five feet? There were lots of starfish and sea anemones, if that helps."

Constable Burns nodded and glanced at Phoebe. "Your aunt said that this cove was the first one you passed as you were going southeast, is that right?"

"Yeaahhh. At least I think so. I remember we got really excited because we saw whales in the distance but we couldn't catch up to them. Alex did, though. At least I think it was Alex because it was a red kayak and that's what he left the harbor in yesterday morning. And he's really fast. There were cliffs all along the water and we eventually wanted to find a place to stop. The cove was the first place we came to."

"One last question, Alice, because I can see the others are waiting for you. Did you notice anything else unusual about the cove? Anything at all?"

Phoebe thought about that as Alice pondered her answer. Had there been anything?

Alice shook her head, "No."

The constable flipped her notebook closed. "Then thank you for your time. I'll let you get back to your paddling expedition. Have a nice time."

Sarah Burns smiled for the first time and suddenly that stern face with the disbeliever's eyes changed and she was just a young woman working alone in a nontraditional job.

"Can I ask you a question?" Phoebe asked. "Did you find out what killed the whale?"

For a moment it looked as if the constable had returned and wouldn't answer, but then her expression turned sad—still Sarah Burns. "From what they could tell in the necropsy, they think she was hit by something—boat, probably. She was pregnant, too. The baby was almost full term." Shaking her head, she turned toward her car. Phoebe thanked her and, pondering the information, she and Alice hurried down to the rest of the tour.

"I'm so sorry about that. My niece found something yesterday that was pertinent to a police case and they needed to interview her before we left." She smiled, but Mike made a point of checking his watch again and there were low grumbles from a few of the tour group. All right. She was going to have to be extra helpful to make sure Alice had a good trip.

"So we were just doing our briefing on the care and feeding of kayaks. Have you paddled before?"

The two of them nodded and donned spray skirts to demonstrate that they at least had that right.

"Ever rolled a kayak?"

She and Alice looked at each other and grinned. "Not well, but yeah."

A little of Mike's resentment fled his eyes. "Okay, everyone. No need to worry. I'm not going to make you all roll your kayaks before we get started. How many of you have kayaked before?"

He started through the demonstration of how to hold the paddles, how to get in and out of the boats, and admonished against dragging the boats over rocks. "My boss tells me that these boats have got to last a season. That means they are worth a lot. And that means that if I catch any of you not taking care of them, you might get left on a beach somewhere. Got it?"

There was a bit of nervous laughter and a lot of head nods.

Phoebe glanced back at Sarah Burns, but she wasn't there, even though her vehicle was still parked. Then Phoebe spotted her climbing into a metal-hulled runabout with a couple of men in blue uniforms and Professor Wilbur. The motor kicked on and the small boat cruised out of the harbor and turned southward, cove-bound most likely.

Mike was assigning kayaks and, to be helpful, Phoebe agreed to paddle in one of the double kayaks this morning, along with one of the other women who was feeling nervous. That left Alice able to have a single kayak, which would likely let her have a closer encounter with whales if they saw any today. She could hope.

Then it was a matter of stowing their gear and all the food and water for the trip in the water-tight compartments of the kayaks. There were a few tense moments as people realized that they might have brought too much, but with Mike's help everything was finally in place. Kayaks were carried down to the water and people waded in. Mike checked their rudder setup and helped pushed each kayak into the waves. Then he was on the water, demonstrating how to paddle—not deep strokes down the side of the kayak like paddling a canoe, but light, dragonfly strokes that used the back and not the shoulders.

"You set the pace," Phoebe called to the woman, Myrna, in the front cockpit. She was a slight Asian woman of perhaps twenty-five, in full makeup, wearing top-end fleece and Gore-Tex jacket that both looked like they were right off the store hanger. Myrna ineffectually dabbled her paddle in the water and Phoebe groaned. It was going to take a lot more power than that to get the behemoth of the double kayak moving. The larger kayaks were cargo carriers and more stable on the water, but they really needed the strength of two people to get a good steam on.

Mike led out of the harbor, the rest of the kayaks like ducklings following, with Phoebe and Myrna bringing up the rear. Phoebe gave paddling pointers to Myrna, but the woman clearly had no idea of the need for power—or she didn't care. Phoebe even tried stopping her own powerful strokes to make the woman pick up the slack. Instead, all Myrna did was place her paddle across her cockpit and complain about how hard it was.

Swearing under her breath, Phoebe dug in and started paddling. If this was her penance for delaying their leave-taking, she was paying it. Thank God Mike had made it clear that they would all have to spend time in the double kayak.

This morning the water carried light swells and the wind in their faces was chill on her ears even though she was working up a sweat. The sun glittered off the water, even though misty clouds still hung over the Broughton Archipelago. In the distance the white coastal mountains hung like apparitions in the sky.

They paddled southward to the music of water gurgling on their hull, the drone of distant boat motors, and the cries of seagulls. A bald eagle—possibly the one Phoebe had seen yesterday—sat in a tall tree leaning out over the water. Two hours out, they coasted past the small cove where she and Alice had lunched yesterday. The silver launch was pulled up on shore and though the tide wasn't fully out yet, three men and a woman appeared to be examining something amongst a bunch of driftwood at one end of the cove. Interesting.

They passed the cove by and continued southward. The trees grew thickly down to the cliff edges at the water. The rest of the kayaks were getting farther ahead and finally Mike came skimming back to them while the others hung in the water.

"What seems to be the problem here?" he said.

Phoebe doggedly kept paddling though her arms and her back were beginning to feel the strain of overexertion. He nodded at her and turned to Myrna. "You're making her do all the work. I want you to paddle like this." He demonstrated.

Myrna tried to emulate him for a few strokes and it eased the strain on Phoebe's arms. The kayak suddenly surged forward. Myrna pulled her paddle from the water. "That's hard."

Mike shrugged. "Well, you can't be expecting Phoebe to do all the paddling and leave you like a queen reclining on her barge. You either put some muscle into it, or you'll be staying on the beach—or paddling your own kayak. Your choice."

With that he turned his kayak and sped back toward the others. Then he shouted and pointed his paddle out into the water. Phoebe followed his motion.

Six tall, black fins cut the water toward the shoreline and the group of paddlers.

Alice would be ecstatic.

Phoebe shouted and dug her paddle into the water. "Paddle, damn you, Myrna!" Heck, *she* was beside herself. She'd come here to see whales. She'd be damned if she was going to let some lightweight, lazy-assed woman keep her from getting up close and personal with them.

Her overlarge kayak wallowed through the waves, Myrna sporadically even hitting the water with her paddles. Phoebe swore under her breath and kept an eye on the fins that were angling closer and closer to the shore. If she could just get the darned kayak going a little faster, she might even make it to see the whales as more than a cluster of distant fins.

Mike meanwhile had reached the rest of the kayakers and had them start paddling parallel to the shoreline. The pod of orca's narrowed the distance and she—she was going to miss them if she couldn't get Myrna going.

"Damn it, Myrna, I could walk faster than this. You want to see whales, you get your sorry ass in gear and use your paddle in the water. Put some back into it!"

It might have done a bit of good. They were getting closer and the pod of whales still hadn't come in along the shoreline. The fins were tall, but one of them was taller than the others, a single huge male who sank below the waves and then surfaced with an enormous blow of water-laden air that glittered in the sunlight.

Please, please, please, let her catch them, but the pod coasted past the kayak bow too far away to really see anything other than low black humps in the water and those fins. The whales looked like they went in close by the cliffs and then they were in and among the other kayaks. Shrieks and oohs and aahs carried back to her as the others pulled their oars out of the water and watched the magnificent mammals slide past.

Phoebe sighed and Myrna—damn her—pulled her paddle out of the water complaining that she'd hurt her shoulder. She spent the rest of the paddle like that, refusing to do anything to help with the kayak. The others sped on ahead following the whales so that, soon, they were simply bright specks on the waves. Finally they disappeared except for one bright yellow craft that came skimming back to them.

Mike.

He must have read their faces, because he didn't say a thing, just slid in beside them and paddled along until they came around a point of land, where a string of seven brightly colored kayaks had been beached on the shore. The other paddlers had spread out, most exploring down the beach, but Alice and another girl had climbed the bluff at the north end to peer down into the clear water. Myrna managed to get her paddle into the water enough to stop the waves from pushing the stern in toward the beach.

Mike, having beached his kayak before them, ran to catch their bow and help Myrna out. Phoebe climbed out herself and marched into shore in time to hear Myrna complain that Phoebe had sworn at her and made her do all the work. If that was what this trip was going to be like, she wanted her money back now, but Mike called to her.

"Could you give me a hand with the boat?" he asked.

Too tired to answer, she slogged over to help heft the bulky craft farther up on the sand beyond the tide line. When they were done, Mike stopped her again before she could just find a log to sit down.

"Listen, I'm not blind. I know what you've been through today. All I can say is thank you and thank God it was you and not some of these—tourists." He caught himself and grinned.

At least someone had noticed.

"Thanks," she said, for some reason relieved.

It made the sunshine a little brighter, the wind a little warmer.

"So I'm going to call everyone and get them to set up their tents, but you might want first dibs on the camping spots. I'd suggest something not too far away from our campfire." He motioned to a spot set back from the water between two large, silvered driftwood logs. She nodded and opened the rear hold of the kayak, hauling out her and Alice's tent, then slogged up the sand to pick her spot.

Tall beach grass grew silver-green around the patches of sand between the stacked driftwood scattered up to the forest edge. She chose a spot that was mostly level and spent a few minutes picking out sticks and stones that could poke into her back, then she set about setting up their tent.

She'd just spread her blue tarp and unrolled her tent with the opening to the front so she could admire the dawn in the morning, when a scream cut through the air and brought her and Mike upright.

Alice—where was Alice?

There. She and the other girl were standing bolt upright on the bluff looking southward. Phoebe spun around. About halfway down the long crescent of beach, a huge tangle of massive driftwood partially blocked the sand. There, a woman was frozen releasing one long, lone escalating cry.

Of course it was Myrna.

Chapter 6

THE DAY FROZE LIKE A SCHOOL EMERGENCY and adrenalin hit her system. Phoebe's attention zeroed in on Myrna. No wind blew. The waves had stopped—at least their sound had. There was only Myrna's strangled keening over and over and over. Then Phoebe could move again.

She scrambled over the driftwood, her tent forgotten, and was on Mike's heels dashing down the beach. She didn't even wonder why she felt the need to do so. Always running in. That was her. Myrna might be a pain in the rear, but clearly she was in distress right now.

Aside from Alice and her friend, the rest of the group were huddled around Myrna. Some were pointing. Others were trying to drag Myrna back from whatever it was that had set her screaming.

The sand dragged on Phoebe's feet as she ran, slowing her down like in her nightmares. If she could just go faster. If she could just get there in time, she might stop disaster; but all the school doors were open and in every one of them Principal Murphy stood taunting. Shaking his head and trying to grab her, stop her from what needed to be done.

No—that was the past! This was infuriating Myrna. This was the beach and kayaking. Her breath tearing her lungs, her pulse pounding in her ears, she stumbled up behind Mike, who had reached the crowd of tourists.

"What the hell's happening?" he demanded.

As one, they pointed.

The ten-feet-high pile of weather-silvered driftwood blocking the beach was comprised of huge tree trunks complete with branches—something lost to the ocean when a cliff somewhere gave way. They effectively made a barrier across the strip of beach. A determined person could wade through the surf to get around it or climb the driftwood-, sand-, and grass-heaped uplands between the beach front and the forest. But the heap of driftwood wasn't so solid that a person couldn't see past it to where the beach continued its long arch. At the moment, seven hands pointed through the barrier.

Phoebe and Mike stepped up to the pile of wood. Upside down on the sand and broadside to the beach lay a red kayak as if it had been thrown there by the surf. On the dry sand beside the driftwood pile lay a man—boy, actually—black hair tangled around his shoulders. Wide-open eyes gone milky, but she knew they were brown. His mouth was open as if in terror of whatever had smashed his head half in. Blood caked the sand around him brown.

"Alex," she breathed and had to turn around. The day felt like a surreal painting. Maybe it was that she was tired from all the paddling, or maybe it was the weird sense that she'd been here before. She blinked. A body on the floor in front of her, horrified students in shock around her, and she had to do something. Could have stopped it from happening. Her legs threatened to give and she grabbed Mike's shoulder to steady herself.

Mike turned a glazed look toward her. His face held the same thousand-yard stare as the rest of the party.

"Mike, why don't you get the rest of them back to camp. What's the name of this beach? I'll call the police and tell them what we've found," she said, fishing in her pocket for her ziplocked phone.

If she could just take action, take control, then the dazed feeling that hovered over her—that had drained their faces—couldn't settle on her, too. She glanced up the beach. Alice was still there. Safe, she hoped—unless someone was still around.

"Would you please keep an eye on my niece?" she asked. "Keep her busy in camp."

Mike blinked. His vacant gaze stirred and found life again. "Right. Aah, this is Longmire Beach. All right, everyone, let's head back to the kayaks. We've got a camp to set up while this is taken care of."

"Wait," she said. "I know I'm not police or anything, but I've been through this kind of thing before. The police would appreciate it if you don't talk about this to each other. They're going to want to interview all of you, most likely. Okay?"

Mike nodded and looked like he understood what she was saying. The others—well, she couldn't be sure.

"Would you point out to Alice where our tent is? Could someone give her a hand setting up?" A gray-haired man—if she remembered rightly, he was named Elliott—nodded agreement. Then they left and Phoebe pulled out her phone. She shot a couple of images just to show what had been found and then dialed 9-1-1. The police picked up and she told them who she was, what had been found and where, and that she'd be waiting for them.

Forty-five minutes later, the metal skiff that she'd last seen in the cove north of here came into the wide bay they were in and headed for shore. Mike waved them down to her and she waved her hands in the air. They beached the skiff beside her.

"Well, look at that. Phoebe Clay. Imagine that. Are you always where there's trouble?" asked Sarah Burns as she stepped off the boat into the water and waded to shore. Dark circles surrounded her sunken eyes and her skin was pale in the sunlight. Her dark hair had pulled loose of her bun and made surprisingly feminine tendrils around her face. Climbing off the boat behind her was Professor Wilbur and two unknown men in the dark blue Department of Fisheries and Oceans uniforms.

"So what've you got?" Constable Burns asked.

Phoebe motioned over her shoulder. "Through there. The driftwood kept everyone away from the body. I took a photo of the scene as we found it. It's Alex."

"Alex?" Constable Burns asked.

"The kid from yesterday morning. The one who found the dead whale."

John Wilbur came up beside them. "Alex Parker? That's impossible."

The first sign of grief: denial. She knew it too well. Had been living it every day until she "retired." Hid out, more like, until she could heal. Not that it had apparently done any good because all the experiences she wanted to forget were sure enough stirring in the dark places in her brain like the proverbial bats.

She shrugged through her numbness. "Have it your way. He's through there."

Burns and Wilbur stepped past her and she finally let her legs give and plopped down in the sand. Rubbed her face and could barely feel her hands. Just sat there, staring out at the ocean. It was gentle how it moved, or you could mistake it for gentle, all smooth swells glittering in afternoon sunshine; but at a touch of the wind, that could all change and the ocean could swallow you before spitting you out on a beach just like this one. Or not, as the case may be.

The ocean was no more a gentle place than a school was. There was darkness under the surface and big teeth waiting. At the moment they were tearing into her insides and she felt hollow and as if all her thoughts echoed.

Burns was beside her again, this time crouched down in the sand. "What time did you find him?"

Phoebe pulled out her phone and brought up her photos and read the time off of them.

"The group must have spotted him maybe ten minutes earlier because that's when the screaming started. It took us that long to run down the beach. Mike was setting up camp and I was putting up my tent. The rest of them were wandering the beach down this way except for Alice and another girl. Then the screaming started." She told how they'd run down there. "You'll have to ask them when they spotted the body, but I'd say it was maybe fifteen minutes before I made the call to the RCMP."

God, if she could just get her brain to work. She felt like her voice came from down a long tunnel and every thought took work.

"Ms. Clay?"

She met Constable Burns' gaze.

"You did good. Really good, keeping everybody away from the scene. You've been through this before, haven't you?"

Phoebe nodded and looked out to sea. "In another lifetime."

Sarah Burns patted her shoulder as she stood up and hauled out her radio and clicked it on. "Dispatch, I'm going to need some help out here. Forensics. Maybe another officer or two. I've got ten people to interview—all witnesses."

She held her hand to her earpiece. "All right, one more officer, but we've got to have forensics. We've got a body and what looks like a pristine crime scene. I'd like to keep it that way until the experts get here."

She listened into her earpiece again, sighed, and signed off. "It's going to be another hour before Ident gets here."

Ident. The RCMP's version of forensics.

"Ms. Clay, why don't you head back to the others? There's no reason for you to stay here."

Phoebe nodded and tried to stand, but her legs had other ideas. "I think I just need to sit awhile. This is bringing some things up for me and I just need to get my head on straight again." She smiled up at Sarah Burns and rubbed her temples. A blinding headache was threatening and that wasn't good. She'd had to take time off school to deal with her debilitating headaches after the shooting. After Rick Hames had died.

She squeezed her eyes shut against the memory of that *empty-eyed young face, and the two others staring blankly up at the school's tiled ceiling. Of blood on the wall and more on the floor, and the halls echoing with screaming as she'd herded students back into their rooms and turned to face the shooter.*

"How do you think he died?" John Wilbur asked anyone who would listen.

"I don't know. From the looks of it, he rolled his kayak. Maybe he hit his head and got washed up to shore," Sarah Burns answered.

Phoebe thought about that response, but something didn't make sense. "How'd he get so far up the beach, then? Why isn't he lying down on the hard wet sand? And why is the sand full of his blood?"

She felt the regard of the others and heard movement as someone stepped up to the driftwood to peer through.

"She's right," Sarah Burns said. "So just how did it go down, then? His kayak's clearly been thrown around by the waves. It suggests he's been here for awhile."

So did Alex's eyes, because they didn't milk over like that immediately. No, Alex had been lying staring at the sky for awhile. She wondered what he was staring at. The stars. Last night's rain. His killer's face one last time before he died. Did he forgive his killer for what they'd done, just liked she hoped—no, prayed—that Rick forgave her?

Damn it, she was losing it here! Turning into one of those walking dead zombies that the school had been full of after the shooting. All the critical incident debriefing in the world hadn't dealt with that. It had felt like the school was a suppurating wound that had grown good clean skin over something that would never heal. It had needed to be lanced to deal with the pressure, but no one cared to release all the bad stuff into the light of day. Not when they hadn't been prepared to do that before the shooting.

So just what darkness was Alex's death hiding? She wasn't sure she wanted to know.

The afternoon had faded to early evening when Phoebe suddenly remembered Alice and staggered to her feet. What was she doing here when Alice needed her up the beach? The girl was only twelve years old. She was all alone and probably scared stiff.

The two fisheries officers sat smoking in the beached skiff. Sarah Burns had made her way around the driftwood pile but had resisted the urge to approach the corpse. Instead she'd walked down the beach away from them, searching the surf line and stopping occasionally to photograph something, then scoop it up and bag it. John Wilbur paced a trough in the sand on this side of the driftwood pile, and out on the water a large blue-and-white boat finally came around the point and headed toward them. Back up the beach, Mike had a campfire going, but the people gathered there seemed to huddle by the flames, as if they were afraid to step away from the light, the warmth. She could use a little of that herself. She was actually shivering. She just prayed Mike had kept Alice safe, because she'd clearly failed in that department. Oh, God.

She nodded at John before setting off, then stopped and came back to him. "Before I go, did you find anything in the cove?"

He shrugged. "No more teeth, if that's what you're asking. We did find a spot with white powder like your niece described. We took samples. There were also some scrapes of paint on the rocks. Red. Blue. Yellow. You scrape your kayaks yesterday? Weren't you in boats those colors?"

"Blue and yellow. Our kayaks were blue and yellow." And Alex's was red. What was this all about? Why was the young man dead? "I gather you knew Alex pretty well."

He nodded, the sun catching on his face, illuminating the sagging flesh of an aging man—still virile, but fading, and he knew it. He must have seen her study for he brushed his hair back from his face in a gesture of the vain. "He started coming in as a kid. His parents and he moved up here when he was ten. I gather he was adopted into a white family and they thought it would be good for him to be near a place with Indian culture. The only thing was, Alex didn't seem to fit in, even though he was native. He once laughed and told me it was funny that he wanted to study whales when his people were from the prairies and had probably never seen a whale. He was bright. Really interested. He started going with me out on the whale census trips, but then he started going out alone in his kayak. He brought back great observations. The kid was good. But there were some problems at the Interpretive Center so I had to ask him to leave."

"Problems?"

"Little things, like missing money from the till and small items going missing. He had difficulty getting along with Meredith, too. I couldn't prove anything well enough to call the police, and frankly I wouldn't have called anyway because I liked Alex, but I had to ask him to stay away." He shook his head. "This is a shame. I always thought that if he just had a chance to grow up and find himself, he'd be a tremendous young man."

A chance to grow up.

He wasn't going to get that now.

Chapter 7

THE WALK BACK TO ALICE SEEMED TO TAKE hours. She tramped the uneven sand and knew she was weaving. Overhead the sky's blue faded and the darkness gathered itself along the distant coastal mountains. Soon the stars would be out and, at this rate, she would still be walking. Something was the matter with her.

The ocean's roar filled her head, even though the waves were barely a foot high when they collapsed on the shore. The wind seemed so strong it could push her around, so that her looping progress made her feel like a drunken woman.

It was taking too long. The day was dying just like that poor boy down the beach. Just like Rick and the others had at the school. Ahead were the fire and Alice and the others and a normal life. That was what she needed. It was why she'd retired. For Alice, she needed to get her head on straight. She stopped and blinked against her vertigo, then stumbled down the sand to the damp track to follow the shore to the campsite. Chill water lapped up over her feet and ankles and that roused her a little. It was smoother here, though still on a slope. Maybe she could manage to not walk like a drunkard.

Night had fully fallen before she arrived, and along the shore the pale green photoluminescence of small plankton flared as the waves fell. The campfire gleamed like an eye burnt in the night and she stopped outside the firelight to admire the tableau of the campfire. Mike had a circle of stones built around the fire and a grill atop them at one side. A pot bubbled with the scent of coconut and curry that made her mouth water. Somehow in the flurry of dealing with Alex, she had forgotten to eat anything. She smelled popcorn and heard soft voices and forced laughter. Alice sat among them.

"Hi," she said as she stepped around the driftwood and into the circle of the living. She felt like she was going to fall down if someone didn't offer a seat. The others couldn't seem to look her in the eyes.

"Aunt Bee. Come sit by me." Alice was up, caught her arm and guided her to a spot where she'd had her jacket resting. Phoebe sank down beside her.

"Thank you." Silently, she stared into the fire. "I'm sorry I wasn't here for you."

"That's all right. I wanted to go to you, but Mike told me you were busy." Alice caught her hand and squeezed. "Was it bad down there?" she murmured.

Phoebe nodded. "It was Alex."

A beat and: "It's so weird. I just talked to him yesterday." Alice's lips quivered as if she'd been holding things together until Phoebe could get there. Phoebe hooked an arm around her and pulled her in close—whether for Alice or herself, she wasn't sure.

"The police will be down to conduct interviews soon," she said.

Mike nodded and stirred the pot he was babying. He motioned to a stack of bowls and pulled the top off a pot in the sand beside him. A burst of steam and the scent of rice filled the air before the breeze tugged it away.

"Dig in, everyone. Best you have dinner before they get here."

"You stay here, Aunt Phoebe. I'll get yours and mine." Alice pulled away from her and it was like losing her only point of warmth.

Phoebe just nodded, conserving her energy for what was to come. Down the beach, floodlights had been set up along the shore beyond the driftwood pile. It made contorted silhouettes of the wood with ghostly shadows laced through the pile as the forensics workers did what they needed to do. Another, larger, police boat sat just off shore in the bay as well, light streaming from its windows.

Alice returned with two heaping bowls, rich with sweet curry and filled with root vegetables. She tucked in, but Phoebe couldn't seem to find her appetite. It just seemed too unfair that she was alive and Alex wasn't. It was too abrupt, too sudden. It made no more sense here than it had before. She needed to understand why this happened, when she hadn't been able to find an answer before. Just thinking of it as a senseless tragedy wasn't good enough anymore—that was media pabulum for the masses and she wasn't one of the masses anymore. She was a survivor.

And that was the thing, wasn't it? As a survivor, she darn well needed answers, because understanding would help keep her afloat. Had to have answers or she was going to drown in the questions.

She gasped for air and seemed to come out of deep water into the cool night air and the warmth of Alice against her shoulder. The bowl was warm in her hand and still leaking the comforting scent. She spooned some into her mouth and chewed, even though her taste buds were dead. Sustenance was important. She could go through the motions.

They were just finishing the meal and sipping mugs of hot, sugared tea when three officers and John Wilbur appeared out of the darkness of the night-bound beach. Overhead, the new crescent moon had risen to tarnish the dark waves along the shore with silver and to catch on the twisted forms of the driftwood and the still-rustling grass between the beach and the forest. The floodlights down the beach polluted what should be a pristine, clear night.

"Good evening, everyone. I'm Constable Sarah Burns and this is Corporal Brett Levesque and Acting Sergeant Marcus Ridley. We need to ask you a few questions."

They identified Myrna as the person to question first, but Constable Burns' gaze found Phoebe across the fire. There were more questions coming.

As people were questioned and released by the officers, they tried returning to the fire, but the silence they shared soon sent them to their tents. Myrna was with them for a long time, her sobbing voice rising up through the darkness until Phoebe wondered where the woman found the strength. At one point in that time, Alice took her bowl and then came back to sit beside her with a marshmallow poked on the end of a stick. She stuck the thing in the fire and laughed when it turned into a torch before them. She blew it out and ate the charred morsel with a child's mixed glee and guilt for finding enjoyment on such a night.

"I'm sorry this has happened," Phoebe said. "I just hope you had some fun today. You did, didn't you?" Please let her say yes. She didn't want Alice to feel the way she was feeling—the way survivors felt.

The girl looked thoughtful. "I saw whales. They were right around us, Aunt Bee." The subject seemed to revive her. "There was one with a fin that was taller than Mike and he was as close as the fire is to us. You should have heard them breathing. It was weird and wonderful and I wanted to reach out and touch them, except I was afraid to." She grinned sheepishly. "If we get that close again, I'm going to try.

"Did you know that just south of here is Robson Bite, where the orcas actually beach themselves to rub their bellies? They run for the shore and slide out onto the rocks and then slide back into the ocean again. Mike said they sometimes swim in close along those cliffs I was on to run along the rocks just below the surface. I was hoping to see that today, too, but it didn't happen."

Still Alice. Still all twelve-year-old excitement regardless of everything that had happened. After all, she hadn't known Alex. But then she paused and frowned.

"Was it really Alex? He seemed so nice. He talked to me a little bit when we were down by the whale while you were talking to the professor."

Phoebe sat up, suddenly alert. "He did? What did he have to say?"

Alice studied her hands, then got up to claim another marshmallow from the plastic bag Mike held and stick it into the flame. It went up with a small whoosh and she pulled it back to admire the flame on the tip of her stick, then blew it out and pulled the charred sticky mass off to pop into her mouth. Sighed.

"He said it shouldn't have happened."

That was obvious. "He said that exactly?"

Alice frowned. "Noooo. It was more like, "It wasn't supposed to be like this." He seemed really upset by Light Fin's death. Sort of like how I felt when Roxy died." Roxy, her blue heeler-German shepherd cross dog had been with her since she was born and had just died last year. "Like he was really close to that whale."

Phoebe thought about it a moment. "I guess he could have been. He could have been out paddling all the time when he wasn't away at school, and if I remember rightly, Light Fin was really familiar to boats from when she got separated from her pod. She hung around with boaters for days until finally some scientists figured out where her pod was and helped her rejoin them. It was a really big deal in the news. There were literally Light Fin homecoming parties all over the province. She really caught the national attention. It's just so sad that it has to end like this. Her first calf was a national sensation because she actually brought it back to the fishermen who first helped her all those years ago as if she wanted to show her baby off." To thank them for giving her back her life.

But it turned out that they hadn't really. They'd just delayed death a few years. Had Light Fin realized that she was living on borrowed time? Had the fact that she lived meant that something else had had to die? Had she heard the waves belling in her orca skull for all those borrowed years?

She scrubbed her fingers through her salt-brined hair and wished for a shower. It was funny that she'd lived through the events at the school, given she'd faced the shooter head on. Was that why she got these strange feelings of impending *something?* She checked her watch. Ten thirty p.m. "You should probably hit the hay. I'll bet we've got another early morning tomorrow."

Thankfully Alice didn't argue. She gave Phoebe a hug and a whispered thank you and headed up toward the tent, her feet squeaking in the sand. "Don't forget to brush your teeth after that marshmallow!"

"Aunt Phoebe, I'm not a kid anymore," floated back through the darkness.

Mike caught her eye from across the fire. He'd been one of the first interviewees and he slid around the flames to sit beside her.

"I'm not sure about you, but a bunch of the folks don't want to carry on with the trip. This whole thing has made them want to go home, and they saw whales today close up, didn't they. Myrna's husband says she doesn't want to carry on. Paddling is too much work and she's traumatized by what happened. He's asked for the two of them to be transported back to Pirate Cove in the police boat. That means we're short two paddlers, and without the second double kayak, we won't have enough supplies for the trip."

"So you're telling me the trip's over before it ever really got started."

He looked down at his hands. "I think I might be able to get the cops to haul a couple of the single kayaks back. I'm prepared to paddle the second double with you if you'll help me get the darn thing back."

Her muscles ached just thinking about it. "And what then? That's it? The end of our vacation?"

"Do you really want to carry on?"

She thought about it. Did she? The thought of getting back in a kayak wasn't all that bad, but there was Alice to think about. The girl might seem all right, but she could be traumatized, too. Better to get Alice away someplace safe. Phoebe shook her head.

"I'm sure the company will refund your money."

She was just so tired and she needed to sleep. She needed to be someplace quiet, where she could think and not feel anymore. The water, with its gurgling kayak hull and its gull cry and the sleek cut of whale fins through the water was supposed to do that—fill her with wonder again and a zest for life. But feeling like she felt wasn't going to make it easy to be in a group. Maybe—maybe this was all for the best.

"Tell you what. I'll talk it over with Alice tomorrow."

She stood up to leave him, feeling caught somewhere between anger and despair, but Sarah Burns materialized out of the darkness.

"Ms. Clay. A word?"

Could this night get any worse? She nodded and followed the constable out of the gradually dwindling circle of firelight until the constable faced her. "Ms. Clay, with this turn of events, we feel that we need to revisit all our interviews. I know you've had a horrendous day, but we'd like to interview you and your niece again tomorrow."

"My niece? But she was nowhere near the body."

In the dim light, Sarah Burns nodded. "Not about the body. About the tooth. We're checking the match of the paint chips from the small cove to Alex Parker's kayak. We'd like to talk to you both about that."

It didn't make a lot of sense to her tired brain, but she nodded. "It looks like Mike is taking us all back to Pirate Cove tomorrow, so we'll be around. Is that okay?"

They agreed that Phoebe would call when they got back to town and she found her way up to the tent. It was lit up from flashlight glow as she reached in for soap, washcloth, toothbrush, and bottle of water. Then she slogged back to the beach. At the water's edge she splashed cold ocean waves onto her face, soaped and spluttered as she splashed her face clean. Then she poured bottled water over her facecloth and wiped the brine off her skin. Better. Livable, even. She brushed her teeth and watched the police officers head back along the water. The ruddy light of the tour group's campfire illuminated only Mike as he set the camp to rights and got ready to douse the flames. She waved good night and climbed up over the low driftwood to her tent again. She climbed inside to the soft snuffles of Alice's slumber.

She barely got her paddling shorts and t-shirt off and her sleeping shirt on before she fell asleep.

Chapter 8

It was a deflated kayaking group who made it back to Pirate Cove after a hard paddle north along the cliffs. A fog had rolled in some time overnight so there was no sign of sun other than the silver light that seemed to fill everything. The mist hung low in the trees and dripped from their branches and draping moss. It covered the logs where they'd sat for a morning meal of strong coffee and omelets cooked in ziplock bags that were boiled in sea water. The mist covered their tents so that for the second day in a row Phoebe and Alice had to pack up a sodden tent. The fires sputtered and spurted and smoked in a swirling breeze that seemed intent on choking them. Phoebe was happy when camp was packed up and they were loaded. The line of kayaks looked truncated with two single kayaks hauled away along with Myrna, her husband, and the body the night before. Traveling with the body should have *really* made Myrna happy. Phoebe didn't envy the police officers on the boat.

Mike honored Alice with the use of his guiding kayak with the warning that her name would be mud if it got damaged. Turned out it was his personal kayak.

Eyes shining at his trust, Alice led the way out of the bay while Mike and Phoebe stayed at the rear to keep an eye on everyone.

Phoebe hadn't yet had the nerve to discuss leaving Johnstone Strait with Alice.

Phoebe never had to phone the police to arrange the interview because, by the time they limped into fog-draped Pirate Cove around noon, the police were waiting for them at the boat launch. So was the media. News vans from both the local island news station and from the big Vancouver television stations were set up along the harbor and down beside the boat launch.

As the kayakers landed, news crews surged forward, poking mikes and questions into people's faces. Phoebe fell back a pace; she'd been through this before and didn't want to have to go through it again. The media were like nematodes—once inside you, they ate you from within. She hid amongst the huddled paddlers but then had to push through them when a reporter and cameraman pounced on Alice. She grabbed her niece and hauled her back as the tour group broke apart into small, hunch-backed parties carrying their gear up through the waylaying camera crews to their vehicles. There wasn't even time for quiet goodbyes—just get out while you could, if you could.

The sudden crowd stole most of Phoebe's hard-won calm. She wanted to climb back in one of these kayaks and be gone. The media could get their hooks in you like whalers got hooks in whales, and just like whalers, they didn't let go.

No, they flayed you in public and boiled away your flesh until there was nothing left of the old person you'd been. She wasn't about to go through it again or let it happen to Alice. She hung back until the others were gone, hoping they would draw away the reporters' attention. It wasn't happening. She had to explain to Alice and get them away.

She grabbed Alice's hand and then left Mike to the unhappy duty of telling his boss all that had happened and that he was pretty much cornered by reporters. Together she and Alice braved the gauntlet to haul their gear up to Phoebe's Subaru. Constable Burns met them.

The good constable looked like she'd been allowed a few hours of shuteye, so the dark circles under her eyes had faded. Of course, with sleep, the veil of police reserve had also fallen back into place. "Ms. Clay. We'd like to interview you and your niece again. Perhaps we could go someplace quieter?"

Great. Just great. And the cameras were already rolling, trained on herself and Alice.

Phoebe nodded, but all she could think of was getting out of here—getting away from the cameras and reporters. They traipsed after Constable Burns up toward her car, but the media just followed.

"Where are we going?" Alice asked.

"Home," Phoebe said.

"What?" Alice stopped dead. "We're supposed to be kayaking." She pulled her hand away from Phoebe's.

"Alice, honey, can we talk about this somewhere else—another time? The constable wants to interview us now."

But Alice's eyes were brimming. "I came all this way to see whales, Aunt Bee. Please. Don't make me go home again."

Phoebe glanced from her niece to the impatient constable. "Would it be possible to conduct the interview later? As you can see, I have a few things to deal with."

Sarah Burns eyed the media crowd warily. Then she pulled out a piece of paper and wrote something down and handed it to Phoebe. It named the coffee shop they'd eaten in and five p.m. "Meet me there, then. Hopefully this madness will have blown over a little."

"Thank you for understanding. We'll be there."

Constable Burns gave a curt nod, scowled at the media, and stalked away with an air that said Phoebe and Alice had better be there for the meeting or there'd be hell to pay. But Phoebe'd survived that sort of threat before, hadn't she? The police's constant badgering. The not giving you time to think or recover. She was not doing that again and she was *certainly* not allowing it to be done to Alice. Thankfully, Sarah Burns didn't seem to be taking that tangent. So far. Phoebe dragged a protesting Alice back to the Subaru.

"Get in the car, Alice." Phoebe dug out her keys and beeped the car open, then dumped gear inside.

Alice shook her head. "No. I don't want to leave."

"Young lady, get in the car. Now." She used her best school teacher command and glared at the news cameras, feeling like a mother bear.

Alice got in and slammed the door. She slouched down in her seat, her arms crossed on her chest and a pout as big as the world on her lip. Phoebe climbed in beside her and just sat there breathing. Then she started the car, dropped it in gear, and drove slowly up through the press of media. Thankfully, most of the cameras turned away, but one was still trained on them and the reporter was looking at her almost in recognition. Not that. Please, not that.

Alice hadn't changed position as they finally left the crowd behind them and the road curved away toward the village and the campground. She took the road to the campground and pulled into an empty spot before turning off the car. Alice threw her a petulant glare.

Scrubbing her briny hands through her salt-stiff hair, Phoebe would have preferred a quiet place to curl up in to sleep and maybe mourn—for the boy, for the whale, for the wreck that this special kayaking trip with Alice was quickly becoming.

"I'm sorry, okay. I didn't want this to happen anymore than you did. I want to be out there with the whales just like you do. But a young man just died, Ali, and it didn't look like an accident. I'm concerned that this isn't a safe place to be. I think maybe we should just forget the whole thing and head back to Vancouver."

"Aunty Bee! No!" Alice's wail filled the car. "I came all this way to see the whales. You paid for the trip and we drove all this way. I don't want to leave. I want to go kayaking."

"But you've already seen the whales..."

Alice turned teary eyes on her. "But you haven't." She sniffled. "And I was so scared the first time that I didn't really get a chance to enjoy it. It's not fair, Aunt Bee. We haven't had the fun we were supposed to have. Yesterday was just a bust—except for the whales. Please, Aunty Bee? Please? Can't we stay? We can go out on day trips and see the whales and visit the islands. Didn't Mike say the whales have a regular pattern of circling through the strait? If you're worried, I'll stay close to you. I'll do what you say. And I won't make a fuss about any of the decisions you make. Please?"

God help her, she was weakening with those watery blue eyes peering up at her. It hurt like heck to see Alice cry, and surely to goodness if they were careful and stuck together, things would be okay. She sighed and scrubbed her salt-sticky eyes. "I'll tell you what. I will try—*try*—to make arrangements for kayaks and a cabin—because there's no way we're tenting with all this media around. If—and I mean *if*—it's possible to do that, I will ask Constable Burns what she thinks. If she thinks it's safe, then we can stay. If not, then we leave tomorrow. Okay?"

Alice blinked up at her, swallowed, and then nodded. "That's fair."

Phoebe had to swallow back a smile; it was so something Alice's mother, Becca, would say.

"All right, then. Let's see what we can make happen. And we need to call your mom and let her know what's going on."

She turned the car around and headed back into Pirate Cove, avoiding the landing where it looked like Mike was still surrounded by media. They parked behind the coffee shop where hopefully the reporters wouldn't notice her.

Beyond the windshield, drifting gauzy blankets of mist wrapped the village of Pirate Cove as if the resort felt like she did and wanted to pull the day in on itself. The white buildings were grey, the other buildings' colors dulled. The Whale Interpretive Center squatted, blood-red and brooding, out on its pilings. The tide was in and the water under the boardwalk looked dark and forbidding. Not exactly the place she'd planned to kayak with her niece.

Alice's breathing had steadied. Her breath misted the inside of the passenger side window as she looked outside. "Aunt Bee, I really don't care what we do. I just wanted to have some special time together with my aunt. You had a rotten time yesterday and now again today, and bad dreams on the beach the first day. Maybe—maybe we should just leave if it'll make you feel better." Her voice sounded so young and brave and like she was giving up everything in the world to do the right thing.

Phoebe had to chuckle a little. "So I take it that you *would* like to stay." As if all the ruckus a few minutes ago could be forgotten. But it was nice to see that Alice could also understand Phoebe's feelings. It was a sign the little girl was growing up, regardless of the emotional turmoil of her age. Phoebe reached over and hooked the kid over to her side of the car in a quick hug.

"You are one special kinda kid, Alice. I don't care what your mom says." She poked her side, teasing.

"Hey. Mom thinks I'm special—at least I think so. And not that other kind of special either!"

"You're totally right. She does. So here's the plan. We'll call up your mom and let her know what's happened and that you're all safe and sound and back on dry land. And while you're talking to your mom and reassuring her that you are fine, I'll see what I can do to get us a cabin and kayaks. Sound like a plan?"

Alice gave a nod and Phoebe pulled out her phone and dialed. The machine burred in her ear across a continent and then: "Phoebe? Hello?" Three thousand miles away, Becca had read her call display and had become anxious.

"Yup. It's me. I just wanted to check in with you in case you happen to see us on TV."

"TV!?"

She held the phone away from her ear and Alice grimaced at the rising pitch of the voice from the phone. "I'm fine, Mom! Everything's fine."

Of course it wasn't, and Phoebe put the phone back to her ear. "I hope you heard Alice. We're both here in all our healthy glory. No wounds, injuries, or blood loss, I promise. Not even a stubbed toe. Nada. It's just that we seem to have fallen into a bit of a mystery. Day before yesterday there was a dead whale on the beach in town and yesterday the kid who spotted the whale turned up dead on the beach we were supposed to camp on. Nothing to do with us, except we were there."

Which was likely why the police wanted to talk to them again.

"We just wanted you to know what had happened in case you happen to catch us on the news. Our kayaking trip has been canceled."

"Oh no! Alice must be devastated!"

Phoebe glanced at her niece, waiting expectantly. "Well, that's what I wanted to talk to you about. We're thinking about staying another few days and doing day trips on three conditions: We can rent a cabin, we can rent kayaks, and the police think it's safe. Sound okay to you?"

There was silence for a moment and Phoebe could hear Rebecca take a deep breath. She could picture her long-haired sister with her tired eyes and her arms wrapped around herself for strength. "She's really okay?"

"She's fine. Great, in fact. And yes, upset that we didn't get our full camping trip. When we're done, I'll give her the phone and she can tell you about the trip so far." She smiled at Alice as Rebecca sighed in relief.

"How are you doing?" Becca asked. "The police. A dead kid. That's got to bring back some memories."

Phoebe rubbed the spot between her eyes. That was the trouble with a baby sister who was too damn close emotionally and too far away geographically. When her world had imploded after the school shooting, she'd taken refuge with Becca across the country; but the media had tracked her down even there. To save Becca and Alice from all the ugliness, Phoebe'd finally returned to Langley, but it was hard to leave Becca's supportive warmth. They'd always been there for each other after their parents died. Years ago Becca had stayed with Phoebe when her marriage didn't work out.

"I'm fine. Just like I said. I can deal with this just like I dealt with things back then."

"But you had to deal with a lot—I mean, are you sure? It took its toll on you, Bee. We both know it did. Are you sure you want to stick around and have the media in your face like last time?"

She squinted out at the camera trucks. "That's not going to happen, Becca. Alice and I are barely involved." She'd keep it that way. "Listen, if Alice and I are going to stay, I need to go try to rent a cottage. Everything hinges on that. Hopefully there's something available. I'm going to hand you over to Alice and let you two have a chat while I go take care of business."

She went to hand the phone off, but heard Becca's "Wait!"

Phoebe pulled the phone back to her ear. "What is it?"

"Alice is really okay? You are, too?"

Phoebe sighed. It was a mom's concern for her baby bird. Phoebe was just an afterthought, except that Becca probably was worried about said baby bird being cared for by a sister who might go off her rocker. Again.

"We're both good. I promise." Tired of once more being tiptoed around, she handed the phone over to Alice. "Talk to her. I'm going to go find us a cottage."

"She's worried?"

"Of course. Now you stay in the car until I come back and don't talk to anyone—not even the police. Hear?"

Alice nodded and put the phone to her ear. "Hi, Mom."

Phoebe slid out of the car and used the key fob to lock the doors against anyone who might try to get in.

She headed to the white building that passed as the resort offices that lay just a few doors down from the coffee shop. The day dripped around her and the air seemed to sigh in the trees as she pulled her collar up against the cool air.

"Ms. Clay?"

The female voice came from behind her and Phoebe kept walking. It wasn't Sarah Burns, so it was no one she wanted to know.

"Ms. Clay!"

Hurried footsteps coming from the boat launch. Phoebe hunched into her jacket and lengthened her stride, but a woman came up beside her. She was petite, dark haired, with lovely golden South Asian skin and Phoebe recognized her immediately as a reporter for the largest Vancouver television station.

"Phoebe Clay. It *is* you." The woman's dark eyes flashed in recognition. "I wondered what had happened to you. Can you tell me what happened on that kayak trip?"

The mist swirled around them as Phoebe kept walking. The sun seemed as powerless to lift the mist as Phoebe seemed to be at outdistancing the reporter. Instead the silver cloud glowed overhead. On the harbor the dark water lifted and fell as if it inhaled and exhaled. The light ting-ting of sailboat rigging against metal masts in the breeze and the hollow clunk-clunk of boats stirring in their moorings were the only sounds. From out on the Johnstone Strait came the droning sound of huge engines, but the fog effectively hid whatever it was from her vision. Ship? Boat? Spanish Armada coming to cause the end of the world? She thought of the old movie about the Russians invading America at a small, east coast town. By the sound it could be happening here.

She paused at the front door to the office to listen to the sound, then turned to the reporter. Mina, that was her name. "I'm afraid you've mistaken me for someone else."

She pushed inside into the glare of fluorescent light and warmth as a headache stabbed behind her eyes. A woman of about forty-five worked at a desk. She had neat, chin-length brown hair that fell in perfect bangs and was pushed back behind her ears, as if to hide the narrowness of her head.

It was like someone had taken a normal face and placed it in a vice, so her narrow nose protruded farther, her eyes crowded the bridge of her nose, and her mouth appeared perennially pursed. She looked up as Phoebe pulled the door shut behind her, hopefully keeping Mina out. The ocean drone, however, still followed.

To either side of the woman's desk were racks of brochures for fishing charters, whale watching boats, and kayak tour operators, as well as a smattering of hotels. An enlarged photograph of an almost still ocean with the Broughton Archipelago and the misted mountains in the background and a red kayak near an orca leaping was framed behind her desk.

The room was decorated in warm pine green and cream—green carpet, cream wallpaper with a fine design of what could be pine trees in the pattern, green venetian blinds currently open over the windows.

"Can I help you?" The woman touched a button on her computer and the screen went dark.

Phoebe grinned. "I hope so. First off, what the heck is that sound?" She went silent and the drone from the ocean seemed to reverberate in the room.

The woman looked puzzled a moment, but then her face cleared. She checked her watch. "Oh! That! That's just one of the cruise ships passing through up the coast. There's a lot of traffic through Johnstone Strait. Freighters. Barges. The cruise ships traveling the inside passage."

Phoebe turned to look back out the window. A lone female figure in a trench coat sidled from foot to foot just outside, but the fog obscured her view of the water. "But I've been here three days now and I've never seen one."

"They usually pass through at night. Less disturbance of the fishermen, and so on."

It still bothered Phoebe that the big ships were there and she couldn't see them, but she turned back to the woman. "Listen,

I'm wondering if you might have an inexpensive cabin for rent. I was just on that kayak tour that got canceled due to the death of that boy. My niece has come a long way to paddle with orcas and doesn't want to go home now, so I'm looking at trying to arrange day trips for us; but with all the media around, I don't feel comfortable tenting." She shrugged, hoping the woman would understand.

Thankfully she nodded. "Terrible thing that. Alex was a good kid."

Phoebe settled in a chair by the desk and glanced over her shoulder. Mina was still hanging around outside, so their conversation apparently wasn't over. "You knew Alex well, then?"

The woman shrugged. "As well as anyone, I guess. He was a real fixture around here. At least he used to be, and then he was every summer when he came home from school. He was one of those kids who didn't seem to really fit in with other young people so he hung out here, did odd jobs for Sam. Worked a bit at the café and spent a lot of time out on that kayak of his." She glanced over her shoulder at the photo on the wall. "That's him, you know. I can't believe he's dead. Now let me see about that cabin. It might be a problem with all the media here and all. They've booked almost everything."

But not all. Phoebe crossed her fingers as the woman clicked her computer screen back on and started typing. Then she scanned the screen.

"How was he killed, do ya know?" the woman asked.

Phoebe shook her head. "No idea. He was just dead."

Eyes wide, the woman looked up at her. "You saw the body?"

Dark hair fanned around his face. Milky gaze at the sky. She didn't want to remember and shook herself, her head, "no." "Just at a distance. The police haven't said anything yet, then?"

"Just that there'd been a body recovered and who it was."

"And that brought all the media?" Phoebe asked.

"Most of them were already here because of Light Fin's death." She narrowed her gaze at the computer screen. "Hmm. All of the cabins in the harbor have been snapped up by the out-of-town news media, but I've got a place that might do. It's just the two of you, right? You and your niece?"

Phoebe nodded and the woman swung her computer screen around. "I'm Lisa Rayburn. My husband and I own the resort."

Phoebe recalled the tall man in the red jacket from her first day in Pirate Cove, and John Wilbur's assessment that the man would likely call the media himself. "Pleased to meet you. Phoebe Clay, teacher, retired. So what have you got for me?"

Lisa's computer displayed a series of pictures of a small cabin. It was a log building, its age showing in the silvered logs, but the other photos showed a snug little one-room place with a small kitchen, a double bed, and a view of the ocean through the trees.

"Just where is this?" she asked.

"It sits up on the bluff up behind the town." She motioned with her arm back away from the water. "There's a road up, but there's also a path directly down to the cove. Takes about ten minutes, I've been told."

It was almost too good to be true. Close to kayaking and yet far enough away she wouldn't have to deal with the media all the time. At least they wouldn't have to be in her face. "How much is it?"

"Hundred and fifty a night. How long do you want it?"

She did some figuring in her head. She had planned to be back home after the five-day kayak trip, but the past three days had been a bust except for Alice's sighting of the whales. The cost of the cabin would be far less than the tour cost for both of them.

"Let's say four days. That gives us four days of kayaking, which was how long we were supposed to be on the trip. But there's a caveat to that. We have to give statements to the police tonight and something may arise that means we have to leave. Can I get a refund after one night if we have to go?"

Lisa Rayburn frowned, then nodded. "We don't usually do that, but after all you've been through, it's the least we can do."

Phoebe signed papers with the caveat added, paid, got the keys and directions and stood to leave, then stopped. "Alex lived around here, didn't he?"

Lisa nodded, but looked surprised. "Why?"

"Well, the first morning we were here Alice met him, and his death hit her kind of hard. I thought maybe we could give his family our condolences." She felt like a heel using Alice as an excuse and she wasn't quite sure why she felt compelled to get the information, but she needed to do it.

Lisa seemed to consider the rental documents on her desk. Then she nodded. "They live in the blue house at the back of the harbor. Hugh and Mary Parker. He's a retired engineer and she's an artist. If you come down from your cabin to the harbor, you'll walk right past it."

Phoebe thanked her and left, jiggling the keys in her hands. With her head down, she hurried past the reporter back to the car, feeling Mina's eyes on her. Asking for the information had been a spur of the moment thing. She shouldn't have done it, should be running for cover instead, but there was something about this situation that had gotten under her skin. It brought up too much for her—things that she hadn't been able to understand, like the senselessness of the killing in her school. Like her role in the shooting and the fact that some wounds just never healed.

Alice, thankfully, had stayed in the car and was waiting when Phoebe got back to her. "Did you get something?"

"Yup. I did. Now give me two minutes to sort out the kayaks and then we're going to town for groceries and then we'll go move in."

Phoebe ran down to Mike, who was loading kayaks onto a trailer. "So here's the deal, Mike. I've arranged for a cabin in town. We're staying four days. Can we have two kayaks for that time? You've seen we can kayak and we know how to take care of the boats."

He nodded. "I thought you might want something like that, so I've made arrangements with Trevor, here, to rent you two kayaks for up to five days." He motioned to the young man who'd rented them the kayaks two days before. He waved.

"Thank you, Mike. Thank you for getting us all back safe and sound." She slipped him a tip.

"Hey. That's not necessary. I should be paying you after all the shit you took—pardon my language. You're a real trooper—something most of my clients need to learn. And thanks for all the help last night. I don't know what I would have done, but you seemed to know exactly what to do."

"Let's just say I've had a little experience with dealing with crime scenes." *Like being covered in one.* She shivered, thanked him.

"By the way, I talked with the tour operator and the rest of your fee will be refunded."

"Even better news. Thanks!" She left him and ran back to the car and Alice.

It was a cheerful afternoon of grocery shopping in Port McNeil, picking up staples that they could use for breakfast and to make picnic lunches for out on the water as well as emergency dinner supplies in case they didn't make it back in time for one of the Pirate Cove restaurants. They made it back to the cabin and found it to be a snug little place that smelled of wood fires and pine resin. The kitchen was small but had a fully functioning stove as well as microwave and fridge. The cupboards were fully stocked with cooking pots and dishes and there were clean sheets and towels and hot water in the shower. Heaven on earth, it seemed. There were board games in the closet but no television.

When they were unpacked, Alice plunked down on the couch. "There's something to be said for a house with four walls—no offense to your tent, Aunt Bee."

"We're missing the ambiance of sleeping surfside like last night, but this is a pretty fair trade-off for a shower." She checked her watch. "I guess we'd better get a move on to meet Constable Burns. She'll probably have road blocks out if we aren't down there on time."

The trail down to the cove was well groomed, but with the fog still hanging on and night falling, it required their flashlights to navigate the steep sections and to make it to the harbor. At the base of the tree-covered hill, a large house was partially hidden in the trees, but the light through the windows and from the front porch light illuminated its blue color. Alex's house, by the color and the fact that a media outlet truck was parked at the street end of the driveway. Ghouls. Ghouls intent on feeding on the body of Alex's family.

"What is it, Aunt Bee?" Alice stopped and came back to where Phoebe hesitated.

"This is Alex's house. I want to give his parents my condolences."

"But Constable Sarah's waiting."

"I know. But tomorrow after the kayaking, we're stopping here, okay?"

Agreed, they carried on to the café where they'd eaten the night before. The place was packed, all the tables full, and Phoebe hesitated before entering. She'd been an idiot not to think of the fact that all those media crews would need a place to eat.

But Constable Burns was waiting and would hopefully hold off the worst of them, so she pushed inside. A few tables looked up and registered recognition of Phoebe and Alice, but as she looked around, she realized most of the people were fishermen or had the look of tourists. Not media.

At a table at the rear of the room, Sarah Burns sat hunched over a menu, her khaki police shirt and a dark blue sweater drab compared to all the bright colored fleece and Gore-Tex in the room. Sarah nodded at them and checked her watch as Phoebe and Alice crossed to her and settled at the table.

"I nearly didn't come in when I realized all the media could be here."

Sarah continued to scan the menu. "I think they took all the restaurant reservations so this is all the locals and tourists. They do a pretty good job here, though."

"We ate here the other night. It was good." And they'd last seen Alex here, through those swinging doors. He must have a summer job here. *Had.* Had a summer job.

"Listen," Phoebe said. "My inclination is to get Alice out of Pirate Cove and back to the big city, but she wants to stay and kayak. Can I get your honest opinion? Is it safe for us to be here?"

Sarah Burns looked from one to the other of them. "I don't think there's anything to be afraid of. Not if you're just tourists."

Was that a stock answer, or was there a warning there? Phoebe chose to take it at face value. After all, she and Alice were snug in the cabin now and they were *only* tourists.

They ordered from the same unhappy waitress with the brown ponytail who had served them two nights before and then Sarah pulled out her notebook and turned to Alice. Low voiced, she asked her about the kayak trip and what happened on the beach where Alex was found and Alice told the truth—that she hadn't seen anything, just her aunt and Mike suddenly start running toward the screaming woman. Sarah took a few notes, but seemed to be focused on watching Alice. When Alice was done with her story, Sarah pursed her lips. "So the day before when you were in the cove where you found the tooth, did you happen to notice anything else, or find anything else while you were doing your beachcombing?"

Alice frowned. "Notice anything? I told you about the white powder. But I only explored part of the beach. There was a bad smell at the northern end. I didn't want to go there and find a dead fish or another dead whale or something." She dug in her pockets and came out with a handful of things that she clumped on the table.

A handful of smooth pebbles, a few small pieces of twisted driftwood, and a fluffy white feather as well as a small silver band. "This is stuff I picked up at the cove and then down at the beach yesterday before…well…before everything happened. Aunt Phoebe hadn't arrived yet, because she had to paddle that Myrna woman."

Sarah stirred her finger into the mix and hauled out the small silver ring and the feather. She picked the ring up and looked at Alice closely, then set it down again. "Any idea what that is?"

Alice shook her head. "Something from a boat, maybe. I found it in a tidal pool in the cove. It was just interesting so I picked it up like the rest of this stuff."

"You found it in the cove? You're sure?"

Alice nodded.

"Do you mind if I hold onto these?" Sarah asked motioning to the ring and the feather as their meals came. Alice agreed so Sarah dropped the silver ring and the feather into ziplock bags and Alice cleared the rest of her debris off the table into her pocket again.

"So is that what this is all about? The whale tooth?"

Sarah met Phoebe's gaze and shook her head. Then she glanced at the rest of the people in the room. "Alex Parker's death wasn't an accident," she murmured, keeping her voice as low as possible.

What did that have to do with this latest line of questioning?

"You think the whale and Alex might be connected by more than his enjoyment of orcas," said Phoebe.

It was what she'd thought yesterday as she'd stood guard on Alex's body. "He was too far up the beach. The sand was totally dry and had been disturbed by wind and footsteps. There hadn't been big enough surf to push him up there if this was a simple matter of him falling out of his kayak and getting knocked on the head. Besides, from what I hear, Alex was an experienced paddler. He'd have his tether line attached to his kayak. If he'd just fallen out and hit his head, they'd still have been connected."

Sarah Burns' eyes narrowed. "You're pretty observant for non-police."

"I—notice things."

"Aunt Bee was always solving the mysteries at her school, like who stole the Canadian flag off the flagpole and who murdered the hamster."

Phoebe froze because the hamster incident had been a precursor to everything that happened. She swallowed.

"Your mother's been making up stories about me again, has she?" She tried to smile, tried to eat her hamburger—the same kind that had looked so good when Alice had one two nights ago. It tasted like sawdust and she had difficulty swallowing. Sarah Burns clearly noticed.

"You both were at the whale's side two days ago. You found the tooth and you were with the group that discovered Alex's body. That's a pretty big coincidence. You were also apparently caught inside the Whale Interpretive Center after it was closed."

"Just what are you implying?" Dammit, it was happening—again. The police were making suppositions that had no relation to reality. "Pirate Cove is a pretty small town and there were all kinds of people at that whale's side that morning. As for the tooth, just why would I turn it in to you if we weren't on the level? And as for Alex Parker's death—well, you heard Alice. We had nothing to do with it until after the fact. We certainly had no idea he would be on that beach. Heck—we didn't know *we'd* be on that beach."

She looked down at her meal, barely touched. Alice had stopped eating when she saw Phoebe get upset. Now she was pushed back in her chair, watching her aunt, who was losing it—would certainly lose it if she stayed.

Phoebe hailed the waitress. "Could we have these two meals wrapped to go, please? Alice, come on. We'll microwave the food when we get home."

Pushing back from the table, Phoebe stood. Sarah Burns looked ready to stand and arrest them. "Enjoy your meal, Constable," she said in the calmest voice she could muster and then she led Alice over to the kitchen doors to await the waitress.

She paid for their food and headed back through the tables, too aware of too many people watching them.

When they got outside, Alice turned to her. "That was *so* embarrassing. What were you doing, Aunt Bee? I'll never be able to show my face in there again!" Alice shook her head and stomped off back toward their cabin.

Phoebe went after her, carrying their half-eaten burgers. "Young lady, you promised that you would stay with me. I expect you to abide by that promise or we're leaving!"

Alice stopped dead so Phoebe almost ran into her. The girl had her arms crossed and avoided looking at her.

Phoebe sighed. "I'm sorry. You shouldn't have had to be part of that. If I'd known it was going to be like that, I wouldn't have agreed to meet with her in the first place."

"She just said stuff that was true. We were there when the whale was found. And I did find the tooth and we were on the same beach as Alex's body."

"And we went inside the Interpretive Center. Sure. It's true, but you don't understand. I've seen this before. They take innocent little facts and turn them ugly and filled with innuendo. They can ruin lives."

Alice turned in the darkness, her pale face like a ghost that caught the light from the harbor in the corona of her hair.

"Why would the police want to ruin our lives? We haven't done anything except go kayaking. Jeeze, Aunt Bee. You acted kinda crazy."

Was it true? Had she overreacted? She searched back through the conversation with Constable Burns and couldn't remember what had set her off. Except for making all those connected observations, Sarah Burns hadn't been particularly hard on them. She sighed.

"I'm sorry, all right? I guess I'm just more tired than I realized. Let's get these back to the cabin, have our dinner, and call it a night."

Maybe if everyone just slept on what had happened, tomorrow there would be answers.

Chapter 9

THE NEXT MORNING CAME EARLY AFTER an uneasy sleep. The cabin couch thankfully made out into a second bed that Phoebe had slept in, leaving the double bed to Alice. The couch had been comfortable enough. It was the dreams that weren't. It was the same old dream of running through a school trying to herd the kids before her while something dark came from behind wearing the face of her old principal, along with a police officer. They were going to kill her—or something was.

She woke in semidarkness to the sound of movement and lay there disoriented for a moment, trying to figure out where she was. The window blinds were dark, so it was still night out—or very early morning. Overhead was a rough wood ceiling with timber rafters. Log walls and the scent of old smoke and pine and—pancakes? A sizzle behind her brought her up and checking over the back of the couch that sat on a braided rug that filled the center of the room. A small light over the kitchen sink revealed Alice pouring what looked like pancake batter into a frying pan.

Phoebe rubbed the sleep out of her eyes. "You're up early."

Alice nearly leapt out of her skin as she spun around, thankfully not sending a spray of pancake batter across the room. "You're awake! I'm sorry. I was trying to be quiet. I really was. I just thought that I'd make breakfast for a change and let you sleep in."

The kid had dark circles under her eyes and worry on her face. Phoebe swept the cozy blankets off and stood, then rounded the couch to give Alice a hug.

"That has got to be one of the nicest things anyone has ever done for me. Thank you." She held on tight to the warmth of Alice's half-grown body and was surprised at the muscle. The girl was far fitter than Phoebe had ever been at that age, but she was still a kid—a kid who was worried. "Listen, I'm all right, okay? You don't need to worry."

Alice pulled away to flip a pancake. "Maybe we should just leave all this stuff with Alex alone and mind our own business."

"I totally agree." Phoebe pulled a couple of plates from the cupboard and stuck them in the oven that Alice had preheated. God, the girl was capable. Then she put coffee on and poured a glass of milk for Alice and fished cutlery out of a drawer to set the table.

When she was done, Alice had two pancakes ready and a third on the way. They sat down at the table and slathered butter and maple syrup over their pancakes.

"Good choice suggesting pancake mix yesterday, and way better than huddling around the camp stove, too," Phoebe said around a luscious mouthful of maple. "You done good."

"Better than porridge every day, anyway," Alice allowed and kept chewing. The silence between then stretched to breaking. "So where do you want to go today?" Alice asked.

It was a simple question, but it was the last thing from casual. Phoebe put down her fork. "Maybe we could paddle out to one of the islands and have lunch and then paddle back. But when we get back, I want to visit Alex's family."

Alice studied her food and stirred the crumbs of her pancake in the syrup on her plate. "Aunty Bee, Mom told me that she was worried about you because of that shooting at your school. She said that having someone else you met die might be really hard for you."

The pancake went leaden in Phoebe's stomach, just as her muscles went rigid. Yes, Alice had known that Phoebe was involved in the horrible shooting at her school, but that was over and done. She carefully set the fork down, furious at her sister for burdening Alice with thoughts that she—Phoebe—was so broken that she couldn't deal.

"Wow," she managed. "Is that what this is all about? Getting up to make breakfast and everything?"

Alice gave a little nod, her mop of blonde hair falling in her eyes. At least she smiled—a small one.

"Honey, I am not going to fall apart before your eyes. I'm a big girl. All the other bad stuff is over and done. I'm just concerned about what's happening. But mostly I just want to spend time with my favorite niece and see some whales."

"Really?" Alice's gaze was misty.

"Of course, honey. That's why I wanted to do this trip."

Alice was out of her chair and around the table hugging her. "You know I'm your only niece, right?"

"That just means you have to work harder to not be the worst, too."

"Aunt Bee!" She pulled back, but she was grinning, and God, it was good to see normal in her eyes. "So I guess I made breakfast and cleanup is your job."

Phoebe swatted her rear and did the dishes and showered—thankfully the water was hot—and came out toweling her hair dry to see Alice with buns and sandwich meat spread on the counter. "You're making lunches now?"

The girl shrugged, but her eyes were too wise by far. "You were busy and it's getting light out. We need to be on the water."

So; not quite normal.

Together they packed the lunch, some bottles of water, a tarp and blanket, suntan lotion, mini first aid kit from the car, cameras, bathing suits, extra warm clothing and rain gear against all possible combination of elements into their day-packs and headed down to the water. Winds during the night had thankfully stripped away the fog, and the eastern sky was orange with nascent dawn while the islands and mountains were still folds of darkness above the strait's glistening water.

When they reached it, the harbor was busy with day charters going out to fish and visitors launching their motorboats to join them. The large whale watching boat in the harbor already had a crowd around it, but two bright blue kayaks waited for them with Trevor. Thankfully, there was no sign of the media at this hour.

"Hey," he said as they arrived. "The boats are over there. We'll expect you back by around five, okay?"

Phoebe checked her watch. Seven a.m. That gave them ten hours, which should be plenty of time. "We're heading over to Hanson Island. That should give us enough time, right?"

He agreed, so she and Alice loaded up and set out again.

The paddling conditions were different once they reached the strait, with a brisk wind in their faces as they turned southward and a good one-foot chop on the water. The kayaks cut through the swells with no problem as their paddles flashed in the angled sunlight. Alice studied the water, probably for orcas, while Phoebe studied the bulk of Hanson Island that sat three miles across the strait. The dark, tree-covered hump of land looked like it had trees coming right down to the water, but there had to be coves there, too, that would be suitable for stopping for lunch.

Just south of town, Phoebe suggested they strike out across the water for the island.

They did, and the wind and waves hit them from the side, buffeting their movement. Phoebe angled them more so that the waves hit them at an angle instead of straight on the side and they began to make progress. It was a tougher paddle, though, with sun and spray in their faces. When they arrived at the island, they were both puffing.

"We did it!" Alice crowed and swiped spray off her face from a recent wave. The sunlight had brought her freckles out so they dusted her nose.

Phoebe high-fived her. Unfortunately the shore here was an unbroken line of trees right down to the water with barely a line of gravel for beach.

"Left or right to find our picnic spot?" she asked.

Alice put on her best psychic prediction gaze and motioned south, so they headed along the coastline into the wind. They passed a larger bay, but the beach area looked like it was mostly large rocks with driftwood thrown up against the trees and Phoebe wasn't really too keen on the way the waves crashed onto the shore. A kayak unskillfully landing in surf could easily capsize, seriously injuring the paddler. They finally came to the end of the island and entered the passage between Hanson and the two islands to its south. The water turned calm and a group of small islands close to Hanson presented some sheltered beaches to choose from. They beached on one of the small islands looking out toward the strait, pulled the kayaks up and spread their tarp and blanket, then set to on their lunch. The trees crowded the little beach they were on, but they'd found a patch of sunlight and were both enchanted when a bird dove straight into the quiet water in front of them and came up with a minnow in its beak.

"Kingfisher," Phoebe named the blue-grey bird with the white whisker-looking feathers and the ragged blue crest. The bird gulped back the fish and dove again.

Alice sighed beside her. "No whales today."

"They're probably taking a rest, all snug down in Robson Bite away from the wind."

They finished their meal and then went exploring the island. It looked like kayakers had used the island as a campsite before. There were signs of campfires and even a lost tent peg in the forest floor, but kayakers were conservation-focused, so there were none of the ubiquitous beer cans and candy wrappers to be found at most campsites.

Across the island there was a long, narrow cove that looked eastward and Alice went scavenging in the pools laid bare by a receding tide while Phoebe climbed through the brush looking for a secluded spot that would stand in for a washroom. Sure, there were places among the tall cedars and fir and hemlock, and the small stands of huckleberry brush and salal, but people might camp there. She kept going and pushed through a tangled fall of tree branches—and found herself on a bit of trail.

She looked back at the branches. They totally concealed the spot where she stood—at least she thought they did.

Good if she was trying to play hide and seek with Alice. A game trail?

She followed the trail a ways and it led to a higher point on the island where what looked like an old eagle's nest sat high in a craggy tree. The area around the tree was clear and showed signs of a fire pit that had been used before. So this wasn't exactly a place to pee either, but frankly it seemed like the entire island had been explored and she *really* needed to find a spot. Giving up on finding a totally private locale, she pushed into the brush to the side of the clearing, stripped down her shorts and crouched, but something caught her eye. Whatever it was gleamed in the sun.

When she was done, she followed the gleam to a patch of tall grass. Dug through the stalks and found a small silver ring. Picked it up. It was just like the one Alice had found in the cove. Odd. This one had numbers etched on it. What was it and what was it doing here?

There was something else caught in the tangle of the long silver-green grass and she eased the stalks aside. The vacant eyes of a skull stared back at her.

Not one. Three. Four. At least a dozen. Vacant eye sockets long cleaned out by decay, sharp yellow beaks jutting out from the skulls. Birds, and not just any birds. Eagles. At least a dozen eagles had died here, or at least their bodies had been dumped here to decompose.

She stumbled back a few feet, but not before she'd caught the gleam of more silver rings and the tangle of bones that were the birds' skeletons. Except for the feet. On all of the skeletons, the talons were gone.

What—the hell—was going on? She gulped in huge gouts of air trying to stop from retching because this was no more natural than a shooter in a school! A massacre. Someone was killing eagles for some reason and this was where they dumped the bodies. Or had. By the look of these skeletons, these birds were a long time dead.

It was the sort of thing that should be reported, but that would just put her and Alice in the police eye again. Not to mention the potential for the media. She hadn't liked how some of the people in the restaurant had been looked at them as they left last night. She'd thought they were locals and tourists, but she could have been wrong. Had that reporter, Mina, told them who she was? If she had, they'd be on her, and she didn't think she could take it again. Not and protect Alice.

But to leave this unreported...

"Damn it!" She fished five more of the silver bands out of the grass, thrust them in her pocket and, feeling like all the light had gone out of the day, pushed back through the trees to Alice.

"So. Find anything interesting?" she asked when she caught up to Alice back by the kayaks.

"Nah. Just a bunch of emptied-out oyster shells and some starfish and sea anemones. I think I might have spotted porpoise out in the channel between the islands, though."

"Really? When?" Phoebe checked her watch; it was still barely one o'clock.

"Just a few minutes ago."

"Then let's get a move on and get going!" She wanted off this island—now. But they had time to explore a bit even though driving the kayak back to the mainland, packing up her car and getting out of the whole north end of Vancouver Island was starting to look like a better and better idea.

Or figuring out what was happening?

Either way, Alice seemed to catch her urgency and they quickly packed up the remainder of their lunch, the tarp, blanket, and any garbage into the kayaks' water-tight compartments, then they hauled the boats down to the ebbing water, climbed in, and started paddling.

Alice led them out of the small bay and into the channel between the islands. The water was barely rippled compared to the strait where foam had started to form on white caps. It was not going to be a great trip home and they probably should be headed back sooner rather than later. What was the saying?

Red sky in the morning and sailor take warning? This morning's glorious sunrise might have been a harbinger of bad things.

As if they could get much worse.

The whole situation didn't make sense. A dead whale. A dead boy, and dead eagles. On the surface they had nothing in common except for being dead. She'd seen that sort of grouping before, hadn't she? *Dead girl and dead boy and dead boy again*—and it was all *her* fault because she hadn't taken action.

"Aunt Bee, look!" A stage whisper and Phoebe had to back-paddle like mad to stop her kayak from ramming into Alice's because she'd been thinking instead of noticing that Alice had shipped her paddle across her cockpit.

Just off shore a group of small dark heads popped up out of the water, and then sleek brown bodies tumbled over each other and dove again to pop up a little farther along the bank.

"Are those sea otters?" Alice asked, eyes shining at the rollicking little beasts in the water. One came up with a silver fish and the rest crowded around to feast on the bounty.

"Just ordinary coastal otters, I think. I don't think there're any sea otters left this far south. Too much traffic."

Alice looked a little disappointed, but not enough so to pick up her paddle. The animals played along the shore and then disappeared up along a small channel. Phoebe and Alice kept going, paddling along the still water between the islands, when Alice spotted a burst of spray ahead.

But there were no dorsal fins cutting the water. Alice pointed and they paddled like mad, never catching up to the low humped shape that surged through the water. Phoebe checked her watch again. Two o'clock.

"Alice, we can't go any farther. It's two and we've got a long, hard paddle ahead if we're going to be back to the cove by five."

Alice nodded glumly. "Can we come out here again tomorrow? If we leave earlier and don't spend as much time on shore, maybe we can explore more of the islands." Hopeful again. That was the thing with kids, they were mutable as heck. One moment the world was ending and the next they could see a bright future. You just had to keep them alive during the dark times.

Together they turned around and headed back through the quiet channel to Johnstone Strait. By then clouds had rolled in and a light rain had started to fall. At least it was a light misty rain in the quiet waters in the shelter of the islands. They paused to pull rain jackets on.

As they exited the island channel into the strait, they paddled right into a squall. The wind and rain swatted them from the south. Waves boomed into their hollow hulls. Phoebe got upwind of Alice to give Alice some shelter.

"Stay close on this side of me," she yelled. Like she'd suspected, this was going to be a tougher paddle and Alice wasn't as strong as her.

Alice nodded and hunkered down to paddle, eyes squinting against the spray, her blonde hair gone dark and plastered to her skull.

Phoebe struck out northward. It would be easiest to just paddle straight north and keep the wind at their back, but Pirate Cove sat across the strait so they had to angle into the waves. Better that than having to broadside them. It would be too easy to capsize. She pointed to a bright bit of sand across the water. "Aim there."

Alice nodded and they struck out.

With one eye on Alice to make sure she kept up, Phoebe set a steady rhythm with her paddle. Progress was slow and the waves slapped them around but they left the island behind and she felt small and vulnerable as they fought for the center of the channel. The thing was, while the wind and waves came from the south, there was a strong current in the water—the tide going in or out, she figured. Either way, it made progress more difficult and after the long haul of driving the double kayak almost alone yesterday, she could feel it in her back and shoulders.

The wind growled around them and waves thudded the kayaks so that the fiberglass trembled. All she could do was keep Alice in her vision and keep going, her mind in neutral. They reached the center of the channel, the current having dragged them backward even as the wind caught their bodies like sails and gave them a push. She increased their angle northward. It felt like someone had given them a boost of speed.

The beach they headed for was almost invisible because the current had pushed them so far south, but she kept doggedly on.

"You okay?" she yelled.

Alice looked up from her concentrated focus on her paddling and nodded. Then her eyes brightened. "Look!"

Phoebe followed where Alice pointed with her paddle. Ahead not fifty feet off their bows, a group of five black fins cut the water heading the same direction they were. Magnificent. One large fin was definitely male, while one smaller fin said they had a youngster in their midst. Where they'd come from she didn't know. She glanced over her shoulder southward and almost screamed.

Like a ghost coming out of the rain, a huge white cruise ship steamed down the center of Johnstone Strait—right at them.

"Paddle! Paddle hard!"

No more paddling at an angle and letting the wind catch them and push them along. They had to get out of the way toward shore and fast.

She turned the kayak sharply out of the ship's path, but could they paddle fast enough? Alice stayed with her as she increased their tempo. The waves boomed against their hulls and buffeted them sideways. Wind caught her paddle and made even strokes more difficult. Spray covered them. Salt stung her eyes. But they had to move.

They left the whales behind and paddled madly toward the distant shore. God help her if anything happened to Alice. She'd never forgive herself. Neither would Becca.

The groan of the wind became the drumming of huge marine engines as the huge ship grew in size. It towered over them. It was going to be a near thing. The rumble of the diesels seemed to erase the world around them. It filled her blood. Her heart beat in unison and they *had to get out of here!*

Huge, white, like a wall about to obliterate them, the ship came on and then it was on them, its high white hull above them so close she felt like she could reach out and touch the gleaming white paint when in reality they were out of the ship's way by a good two hundred feet. The huge bow wave picked them up and drove them shoreward and she paddled to stay on it as long as she could. When it passed away from under her, she glanced back. Alice was still with her, still glued to her side. The ship had passed and figures stood at the stern rail waving. Alice waved back. Below the railing, barely thirty feet off the water, a small deck stood exposed to the elements. There, in the rain, stood a man in a white uniform. He looked like he was smoking. He didn't wave.

"The whales!" Alice cried and pointed. The pod of orcas had traveled northward faster than Phoebe and Alice could travel and had stayed in the center of the channel—right in the path of the ship. As they watched, the whales seemed to recognize their peril and veered off toward the shore at the last minute.

"I wonder how many don't veer off in time," Phoebe said and set off again. The ship's bow wave and wake had pushed them far closer to shore. They came in close to the cliffs in another thirty minutes and rafted up together for a short rest and a drink of water.

"Do you think that's what happened to Light Fin?" Alice asked.

"What are you talking about?" Phoebe took another swig of water and settled the bottle back within reach under the bungee lines on the bow.

"You wondered how many whales don't veer off. If they don't veer off, they get hit, don't they? Like maybe that's what happened to Light Fin."

The white behemoth traveled northward, its huge propellers churning the water behind it, the groan of its engines filling the strait.

"Could be."

And the thought filled her with horror, for the ship hadn't even slowed down though they were clearly right in front of it. Would it have hit them, too, if they hadn't gotten out of the way in time?

Chapter 10

THEY MADE IT BACK TO PIRATE COVE BY FIVE thirty, signed in their kayaks with Donnie and said they'd be back tomorrow pending the weather, then bundled their stuff back to the cottage. When they'd both showered and changed, wearing their hooded Gore-Tex against the rain, they trudged downhill—ostensibly for dinner, but at the base of the hill Phoebe stopped before the blue Parker home. The media van was at least gone.

Well, she needed to get this done. She headed toward the house, Alice following, rolling her eyes.

The house was well kept, the shake walls recently stained, the white trim around the windows newly painted. On the single concrete step, a copper planter stood burgeoning with red and white geraniums that seemed to glow in the misty air. The brown wooden door had a brass knocker shaped like a cat's head.

Use it? Actually call on the family? It was the one thing she hadn't been able to do before, and that was part of her shame. It hadn't just been the school district's instructions that she was not to make contact, it had also been shame that she hadn't been able to stop the whole thing from happening. She should have seen it coming. Well, she had nothing to be ashamed of this time, did she? She used the knocker on the door.

For the longest time no one answered. She saw a curtain stir in what must be the living room, and then heard the sound of footsteps behind the door. It opened a few inches to release the scent of rich tomato sauce and to reveal the eye of a woman of perhaps fifty.

"Yes?" she asked. "May I help you?" She had clear blue eyes, but there was strain around them and a downturn to her lips that looked like a new expression to her.

"I'm sorry to bother you, but I'm Phoebe Clay and this is my niece, Alice. We're just tourists passing through, but we met your son, Alex, our first morning here and saw him out on the water. He and Alice spoke and we wanted to pass along our condolences for your loss."

She felt the Parker woman's study and then the woman sighed and opened the door farther. She was a pretty woman, though her looks were fading with age. She had grey-blonde hair pulled back in a ponytail, and wore a chambray shirt loose over paint-stained jeans. She peered out at the street.

"Thank you for your kind words. The media truck must have just left." She pulled the door farther open and stepped aside. "Would you like to come in? You don't look like you're with them. You look like you've been out paddling today—I can tell by the windburn. Perhaps we can have a cup of tea? Or have you eaten? I have dinner almost ready."

Well, in for a penny, in for a pound, and she *did* have a few questions. She glanced at Alice, ignored the girl's urgent head jerk toward the road, and stepped into the house. Alice gave a small groan and followed. Mrs. Parker pushed the door shut behind them.

"The darn reporters have been out there all day. There were more earlier, but most of them left when the police did." She shook her head. "Call me Mary, everyone else does."

They stood in a functional little front entrance with what looked like an antique, spindle-back bench by the door so you could sit to take off your shoes. Shoes lined the wall under the bench, and wooden peg hooks burdened with various coats and jackets lined the other side of the entrance. She hung their jackets there and they left their damp shoes and followed her into the house.

It was a snug little place, with a small living room to one side of the entrance and a formal dining room to the other. The living room was filled with a comfortable overstuffed couch and chairs in navy blue and forest green that faced a stone fireplace that looked like it still burned wood. Smelled like it, too, for that matter. Above the fireplace, a large split log, supported on stone struts, formed a mantel that held framed family pictures and what looked like two old hurricane lanterns.

The dining room had green floral wallpaper over wood wainscoting and what looked like an old mahogany table and chairs. A bowl of ornamental fruit filled the center of the table under a small crystal chandelier.

Mary Parker led them past the two rooms and into a kitchen at the rear of the house. Light seeped in through a bank of windows that looked out onto a small lawn surrounded by dripping coastal rainforest. The room was painted bright turquoise with white cupboards. At one end sat a nook padded with yellow cushions, the table set with two place settings. A double sink sat under windows that held a small kitchen garden, and a sliding glass door gave onto a small patio with a small glass table and chairs and a number of pots filled with more flowers.

On the white stove bubbled a large vat of spaghetti sauce and a batch of pasta. Mary stirred the pot of sauce and checked the pasta. "You will have dinner with us, won't you? I think I've cooked the same amount I always used to, but with just the two of us..." Her voice broke and she leaned on the counter and rubbed her eyes with her fingers. "I'm sorry. I just don't know how I'm ever going to believe that Alex isn't going to just walk in the front door again."

"I know this is a painful time, Mrs. Parker. Perhaps this isn't a good idea. I—we really didn't want to intrude or to impose on your hospitality."

Alice gave her a look that clearly said she didn't believe her.

"Nonsense," Mary said. "If Alex was alive, you'd probably be here. He was always meeting interesting people and inviting them home. He knew I always cooked extra. Besides, having a normal dinner conversation would be a nice change from sitting and staring at the food. Now perhaps you, young lady, can help me out and set some extra places at the table?" She pointed out the cutlery drawer and where the placemats were and Alice hurried to obey while Phoebe strained the pasta and poured it into a huge bowl. Mary ladled the rich meat sauce over top and then set the pasta bowl and a bowl of parmesan on the table.

"Hugh," she called. "Dinner! And there's company."

Somewhere in the house a door opened and shut and footsteps clumped heavily down stairs, then a second door opened into the kitchen and an elderly man stepped in. He must have been fifteen years Mary's senior, with steel grey hair that must have once been almost black. He had coal dark eyes and a lean ascetic face that took in Phoebe and Alice's presence with two parts suspicion and one part surprise.

"Who's this, then?" he asked, pausing in the doorway that gave onto another hallway.

"Hugh, this is Phoebe Clay and her niece Alice. They came to give their condolences for Alex. Apparently they met him their first morning in the cove." If her voice was bright, her welcome still didn't seem quite natural.

Hugh, however, frowned. "So they said their 'sorries.' What are they doing in my kitchen?"

Alice cowered back toward the door to the front of the house and Phoebe felt like doing the same. They shouldn't have come. Shouldn't have intruded on the grief in this home.

"They're staying for dinner, of course," Mary said and turned back to the stove and gripped its sides. "Alex would have brought them home. He always brought home the people he met."

"I'm terribly sorry, Mr. Parker," said Phoebe. "We had no intention of intruding. We really had no intention of staying, but your wife insisted." Phoebe edged toward the door, motioning at Alice to follow her.

The man's gaze darted toward her, the wound in his eyes almost intolerable. Then his gaze flickered and the line of his lips seemed to soften. "So you aren't one of those bloodsuckers from out front, then?"

"Media? Definitely not. We're just a couple of kayakers." But she still sheltered Alice behind her. Was this how it would have been before? Worse probably, because she'd been nowhere near an innocent bystander then.

Hugh Parker sighed and his shoulders slumped. "Accept my apology, Ms. Clay. I'm sorry. It's been a hell of a few days. Please join us for dinner." He crossed the room to his wife and put his arm around her shoulders. "It would be far better than the two of us just staring at each other."

Alice was tugging at Phoebe's shirt, urging her to leave, but darn it, this might be a way to get some information that could help her understand what was happening. Ever since she was a kid, she always wanted to understand why the world worked as it did. That was why she'd studied science in school. It was only after she'd become a schoolteacher that she'd realized there was more to how the world worked than the science—there was the people.

"Alice, honey, why don't you go wash up and I'll serve us both."

She shoved Alice to the kitchen sink and slid into the nook with Hugh on one side of her. Alice washed her hands and then slipped on the other side of her and Mary took the chair. Mary served herself and Hugh and soon they were eating spaghetti with fragrant tomato meat sauce. After the day she'd had, it tasted like heaven.

"So how did you meet Alex?" Hugh asked as he wound spaghetti onto his fork.

"It was actually Alice who spoke to him. We were down at the harbor with the dead whale Alex found. He and Alice got to talking."

Mary set her fork down and bowed her head until Hugh caught her hand. Squeezed.

"He loved that whale like she was a kindred spirit. Light Fin this and Light Fin that. He was just a little kid when she was found, and we took him out on our friend's boat to show him. He took a shine to that whale like I've never seen. The kid had a dog at the time, but it was Light Fin all the way. She was lost and away from her kind and I always figured he thought they had that in common." He shook his head and Mary met his gaze, her eyes too-bright with tears.

"Alex was always such a lonely kid," Hugh said. "We adopted him when he was a baby. None of the white kids wanted to hang with him and the Aboriginal kids—well, he wasn't enough like them, either, coming from a home like ours. So as soon as he was old enough he wanted his own kayak and spent his days out on the water—with Light Fin alone and then after when she rejoined her pod."

"He was such a good boy." Mary rubbed her eyes. "He was determined to study whales when he grew up." Her breath shuddered as she sighed. "I just can't believe he's never going to walk in that door again and tell me about all the wonderful things he saw today."

"He—he was really upset about Light Fin." Alice's voice sounded small in the room.

Phoebe smiled at her and caught her hand. "Maybe you can tell them what he said to you."

"He said it shouldn't have happened. He was mad and sad and—and disappointed. He said no one really cared about the whales anymore except as tourist attractions or circus animals." A single luminous tear formed at the corner of her eye.

"From what I've heard, he was a very bright young man. Someone you must have been very proud of," Phoebe said.

"What I don't understand is why anyone would do this. Why kill our boy? He loved whales. He was good in school. We had arguments at home, sure, but they were normal. He was just a kid with dreams."

Phoebe closed her eyes because the words echoed so many things said before, so many things she'd heard on the news, in staff rooms, in eulogies. She thought of all the strangeness of the past few days. All the things she'd seen and heard.

"Mr. and Mrs. Parker, did your son have anything to do with eagles?"

The Parkers stopped eating and looked at each other and then at Phoebe.

"Why do you ask?" Hugh said, sitting back in his chair. The suspicion was back.

Phoebe took a deep breath. "I ask because an eagle band was found on the same beach where a whale tooth was found. I just wondered if he was interested in them, too."

Hugh shook his head. Mary gave a weak smile. "Eagles weren't his interest—or they hadn't been for years, but a few months back I noticed him reading some articles about them. It was mostly articles that he'd pulled off the net."

Interesting. "Did you happen to notice what articles they were? What they were about? Do you still have them?"

The look on Hugh's face said she had erred in questioning them. A true innocent here to give their condolences wouldn't ask this kind of thing. "I'm sorry. It's just that I'm trying to understand what's happening. Why was a fine young man like Alex killed?"

She couldn't comprehend it. Still couldn't, even though God knew she had tried. It was so senseless that it couldn't really be explained, but there had to be some rhyme or reason here. A logic behind it, even if it was wrong-headed. Even a senseless shooting in a school had a misguided rationale behind it. But this was a different kind of crime. It had to be, or else she didn't know if she could stand being part of a world where people were killed for no reason.

"So you don't believe it was an accident, either," Hugh said, voice shaking. "Those damn police were here and they wouldn't say one way or the other. They said they wanted to finish their autopsy and then they'd let us know. It felt like—like they wanted to blame Alex for being out there, for doing something careless and for dying. But I know. I know Alex. He was a skilled kayaker. He was careful. It was no accident that killed my boy."

Odd. Sarah Burns had said Alex's death wasn't an accident. Why change her story with the Parkers?

Hugh's voice rose as he spoke and then he slid out of the nook, stood, and walked out of the room. His footfall was heavy on the stairs and then he was gone in the slamming of a door upstairs.

Mary looked at her half-eaten meal and began to gather the dishes for clearing. Phoebe sprang up to help her as Alice scooped a couple more mouthfuls of food into her mouth.

The room was silent except for the clatter of dishes. Alice sat like a dazed rabbit in her side of the nook as Phoebe went through the motions of helping Mary clean up. Dishes in the dishwasher. Food poured into a large bowl for the fridge. How many days would they be eating it? Judging by how little the couple had eaten today, it would keep them in dinners for a week at least.

When she was done, she thanked Mary for dinner, excused herself, caught Alice's hand, and hurried to the front door. They pulled on their jackets and shoes and were about to leave when Mary came after them. She had an envelope in her hand that she handed to Phoebe. "The police took pretty much everything—except this. It got left on our printer by mistake. Alex was having trouble with his computer printer so he must have forwarded the document for printing in Hugh's office. If—if you find out anything about what happened to our boy, please let us know."

Phoebe caught her in a hug. "I will, Mary. I will. I promise."

Then she opened the front door and led Alice out into the rain. The media truck was back at the end of the driveway.

Chapter 11

Outside, the rain came down in a steady downpour. The light was fading and the wind rocked the trees so branches thrashed and the trunks groaned around the blue house as if they were women in mourning. Phoebe looked back at the blue house hunkered down against the night. Against life, more like. Alice had her head down under her hood and she was stomping away like she was mad. Phoebe sighed. She'd been an idiot pulling the girl into that household. She should have just expressed her condolences and left.

She hurried to catch up to her and caught her shoulder. "Alice? Alice, you okay?"

The girl jerked away, glancing up with tears in her eyes, her thin body shivering. She clutched her body as if she was freezing and started toward the path back to the cabin. Phoebe let her go.

"I'm sorry." But the wind took her words away. She started after the girl.

At the street, the news station van's cab door opened to expose a woman in a red Gore-Tex jacket, the hood pulled up over dark, perfectly coifed hair. Mina. Phoebe stopped dead in recognition.

"Hello again, Phoebe. Seems like maybe you're more than a bystander this time, too."

Phoebe almost froze, but that was what the woman wanted, wasn't it? Get her to pause long enough that she could be cornered—sort of like hunting at night by shining a light in deer's eyes to blind them. She knew what it was like to feel hunted. The Parkers must be feeling the same. And now Alice. She had dragged the girl into this warped world. Phoebe pulled her hood a little lower and went after Alice. She didn't have time for the bloodsucking creatures of the media—not even the ostensibly good ones.

The trail up the hill was dark through the forest, but Alice didn't use her flashlight. Though Phoebe tried to catch up, clearly Alice didn't want her to. By the time they reached the cabin, the girl was almost running. Of course the door was locked and she fell against it crying. Phoebe caught her, pulled Alice into her chest.

"I'm sorry. I'm sorry. I'm sorry." It wasn't enough by half. "I thought it would be okay to just have dinner. I don't know what I was thinking." She looked up at the blackened treetops and the rain smacked her face. "I keep forgetting you're only twelve, Alice. I wanted to know about Alex. But I shouldn't have dragged you into it. I was wrong. I'm sorry you're hurting."

"Those poor people. They hurt so much. That house just aches."

Out of the mouths of babes...

Phoebe unlocked the door and ushered Alice inside. Got her settled on the couch and made hot chocolate with marshmallows in two mugs, then sat down beside her.

"I was stupid going there. I hurt those people and, more importantly, I hurt you. It will not happen again."

Alice brushed her mop of blonde hair out of her eyes. "The Parkers said the police aren't sure if Alex died by accident or was killed, but Constable Burns said his death wasn't an accident. I don't understand, Aunt Bee."

It was surprising that Alice had picked up on that inconsistency. "The Parkers also said they didn't believe it was an accident because Alex was so careful and so good at what he did." She sipped her hot chocolate and almost burned the roof of her mouth.

Alice blew on hers and sipped. "Mmm. Good. Thank you." The flush of tears was clearing.

"Listen. I really am sorry. I won't do anything like that again. I promise."

Alice met her gaze, and for a kid, her gaze was far too steady—and filled with doubt. She'd been disappointed by adults before and had already come to the realization that there'd probably be a next time.

Phoebe sighed and sat back against the couch, shaking her head. "Okay. So maybe I will. There's something going on here, Alice. Something weird. I found something out on that island today when I was looking for a place to go to the bathroom." She went to her jacket and fished out the few silver bands she'd collected, five of them in the palm of her hand. She held them out to Alice. "'Recognize them?"

"They're like the one I found in the cove with the whale tooth."

"That's right. But I found these with something else so I know what they are. They're wildlife leg bands from eagles." She told her about the bones and Alice's lips quivered and she took a gulp of her too-hot cocoa and then cried outright.

Phoebe gathered her in her arms and pulled her into her chest. "It's okay. It's okay. I've got you, baby girl."

"It's not okay. It's awful. Someone's killing eagles. Why would someone do that?" her voice was muffled against Phoebe's shoulder and Phoebe stroked her hair.

"I don't know, honey. I don't. There must be some money in it, or something. The good thing is those bones looked like they'd been there for awhile." But not long enough. Things would decompose quickly in this kind of weather and terrain.

Alice sat up and scrubbed at her eyes. "You—you're trying to solve it, aren't you? You're trying to solve the mystery. That's why we went to the Parkers."

For a moment she wasn't sure how to answer. Solving a mystery hadn't been how she was thinking about it. It also wasn't why she'd gone to the Parkers. She really had wanted to apologize—it just all got a little away from her.

"I want to understand." Needed to understand, more like. Because if she could understand this death, maybe she could understand what had happened before. How it had happened. How and why so many lives were, if not ruined, at least changed forever.

"So—so maybe we can work on it together? We can solve the case together?"

Phoebe studied Alice's young face. So eager. So determined. So filled with trust just like all the rest and...

She had to look away. "Let me think about it, okay? Your mom wouldn't want you involved with this at all. Alice, maybe you should go home and then I'll come back and see things through for the both of us. Your mom would not like you at risk."

"I'm not at risk. I'm with you and we're not doing anything dangerous—just going paddling, right? Mom doesn't need to know. Besides, if we solve the case, mom will be really proud, won't she?"

"We're here to kayak, not solve a mystery. A boy was killed, Alice."

"You think I don't know that? I might not have seen the body, but I know he's gone. I talked to him and now I have to keep telling myself that he's not anywhere in the world anymore. Do you know how weird that is?"

Her voice broke and so did the dam on her tears. She hunched on the couch, shoulders heaving, her hands covering her face.

"Every time I close my eyes, I see Alex's face. It's like he's trying to tell me something and I just can't hear him, Aunt Bee. I need to understand what happened to him."

Phoebe winced as her stomach lurched. The damage she'd been afraid of had already been done. Alice was face-to-face with death and she had to come to terms with it. Would sending her home do that or just leave her unable to deal with the nightmares?

Alice sniffed and wiped her eyes. "What'd Mrs. Parker give you, anyway?"

Phoebe shrugged. "She said it was something Alex printed on his parent's computer. That's all. We don't need to look at it." At least not right now.

"Aunt Bee! That's not fair. I want to help find Alex's killer, too."

"No. Not going to happen. I'm going to turn those bands over to the police and we're going to focus on kayaking. Now how do you feel about getting your behind whipped at cards?"

They played gin rummy and drank cocoa until it was time for bed. The cabin was toasty and warm because Phoebe even managed to get the fire started, so that they sat on the rug with their refilled mugs of cocoa and their playing cards before the hearth. At nine-thirty both of them were yawning like all get out, so they folded out the couch and Alice went to bed.

By the time Phoebe came out of the bathroom from her nighttime ablutions, Alice's breathing had evened out into the sleep of the utterly exhausted. The girl lay spread-eagled on the bed, the covers kicked down around her feet, her pink shorty pajamas and smooth pink skin exposing just how young she was. And vulnerable.

Phoebe had to keep her out of this. Had to get out of it herself, even though she was sure she could figure out what was going on and that figuring it out would somehow make what had happened at the school more comprehensible.

She went to her coat to fish the envelope from Mrs. Parker out of her coat pocket. It wasn't there. She whirled around to the bed and Alice. A piece of folded paper and an envelope lay on the floor by the wall. She scooped it up, furious, and yet a part of her was relieved.

Alice knew. Alice was part of this. She didn't have to keep secrets. She settled at the small kitchen table to read it.

It was off the internet and wasn't so much an article as an advertisement. It was off one of the largest e-commerce sites in the world and held a listing for ritual supply houses. Voodoo. Hoodoo. Wiccan. What the heck?

She scanned down the page and stopped at a listing. *Specialty ritual items: American Indian objects, genuine eagle feathers and claws.*

All those eagle skeletons and no feet. The cabin suddenly went cold. She remembered it now. There'd been a series of finds of eagle carcasses near Vancouver a few years back. She remembered the horror of her students at the crime. The news had never reported the capture of the culprits.

Nope, they'd moved on. To places like this where there was far less chance of being found.

She went back to her jacket and fished out her phone. Call Constable Burns and tell her what she'd found or keep it to herself?

If she called Burns, there'd undoubtedly be more questions of both her and Alice. She looked over at the sleeping girl. She was not putting her through that. No, she'd quietly ask around and if she found out anything by the time they left town, she'd pass the information on to the police.

The question was where else to ask that would help bring closure for Alice and still keep her safe.

Still asking herself that, she went to bed and joined Alice in the sleep of the dead.

Voices and faces. Rick Hames in her classroom, held after class one more time for yet another outburst. Behind him stood a girl who was crying—his younger sister, Jennifer. Rick was a slight kid. A bright kid, with a too-long thatch of unkempt brown hair and too-dark eyes that always seemed half an inch from despair. One of those always described as having a chip on his shoulder. In fact, what he had was a learning disability that had left him functionally illiterate going into grade ten. That was when the wheels really fell off his schooling and he started getting in fights—usually on the receiving end.

She was at her desk and Rick was talking to her from three feet away but she couldn't hear him. She knew something was wrong because he was crying, too, but in anger—rage, even. He was punching her desk and she could feel the vibration through her hands that rested on the desktop, but when she tried to get up, to go to him, something glued her to her chair, glued her hands to the desk.

She would talk to him, but no words came out of her mouth. Instead a cloud of dark roiled out from between her lips to fill the room and Rick was caught in a last circle of light. Nothing she could say. Nothing she could do. Anything she tried was just going to make it worse and her chest tightened because she knew it was going to get worse. Had gotten worse because no one would listen—until Rick took matters into his own hands, didn't he? He found the weapon when all his requests for help didn't work.

And behind him through the roiling dark smoke, Jennifer was still crying as Rick faded away into that cold, cold light.

She woke up gasping into semidarkness. She'd failed Rick and she'd failed Jennifer. Her heart pounded so hard it hurt. But Rick's death was a year ago.

The cabin. She was in the cabin with Alice, not trapped in a classroom unable to help a boy who was to become a double murderer. She lay there, staring up at the ceiling, listening to Alice trying to be quiet as she carried her things into the bathroom to change. When the bathroom door clicked shut, Phoebe's heart rate was almost back to normal. In her sleeping shorts and t-shirt with a fleece pulled over it, she turned the radio on for the news, put the coffeepot on, heated a pot of milk for Alice's cocoa, and stirred up a batch of oatmeal. It was ready when Alice came out of the bathroom and they sat at the table together in silence as the radio news blathered on about the stalled investigation into the missing north island girls.

Both of them went still when the news shifted to the mysterious death of a young kayaker on the northern Vancouver Island coast. The police had announced that it was accidental.

Both of them looked at each other. Phoebe shook her head, disbelieving.

"Why did they change their story?" Alice asked. "I don't understand."

Phoebe didn't understand it either.

The news moved on to sports reports about the Vancouver Canucks hockey team and local basketball team.

Phoebe finally sighed and set her spoon down. "This is early enough we should be able to get over to the islands to have a good while exploring."

"Maybe the weather won't be good enough. If there's a storm like yesterday, I don't think I want to go," Alice said into her half-emptied bowl of maple-syrup-drenched oatmeal.

"It doesn't sound like last night. Leastwise the wind has died down." Last night she'd gone to bed with it whistling through the treetops. The trees had groaned.

As if on cue, the weather report came onto the radio—a clear day.

"Looks like it's a paddling day." Phoebe sipped her coffee, having finished as much of the oatmeal as she could stomach. It wasn't a lot. Her stomach for food just seemed to have faded the past few days.

By five she was showered and dressed and, hair still damp, on foot they packed lunch and their gear down to the nearly empty boat launch. In the coming dawn, Trevor was there again, but not alone. A dark-haired girl was talking to him and when she turned around, Phoebe recognized the sullen waitress from the restaurant. The way her face shut down, she didn't seem any more friendly when she wasn't working. Her conversation with Trevor ended.

"Morning!" Phoebe put on her best cheery morning voice, even though she felt like she'd been run over by a truck, and stuck out her hand. "Phoebe Clay. I think you've been our waitress a few times. This is Alice, my niece."

The girl left her hand hanging and turned back to Trevor.

"You think about what we talked about." Then she marched past them up the hill.

"Sorry to interrupt. We just wanted to get an early start," Phoebe said.

Trevor was still watching the girl march up the boat launch. His expression wasn't happy.

"Trevor? You okay?"

"What? Yeah. Sure." He scrambled away to produce their two kayaks from behind the boat launch office.

"Girl trouble?" Phoebe asked as he helped her and Alice load up and shift the kayaks down to the water.

"Sister trouble," he murmured and shook his head, clearly not wanting to talk about it.

"Trevor, can I ask you a question? Has there ever been a problem with eagle poaching up here? I know there was an issue in Vancouver a few years back. A lot of birds were slaughtered. I was out paddling the other day and saw an eagle and it reminded me of what happened down south."

Trevor pursed his lips as if he was thinking, but he didn't meet her gaze. He shook his head. "Not that I can recall, and something like that—we'd notice. There're a lot of eagles up here and they're part of the experience of coming to Johnstone Strait."

"Funny. I've only seen the one since we've been here. Just unlucky, I guess. I sure hope the weather holds today. Yesterday we almost got stuck over at the island and then we nearly got run over by a cruise ship. Say, you don't happen to have a schedule for the big boats, do you? I'd love to know when we have to watch out for them."

He thought a few minutes. "I think you're okay for today. Yesterday was Holiday Queen, so there's usually a break of a few days."

"Is there a schedule?"

"Well, sure."

"Can I take a look? Not that I don't trust your memory and all." She tried for an ingratiating smile and he finally shrugged and went back to the office to return with a tattered and torn brochure with a list of boats and times. She opened it up, but he stopped her.

"You don't really need to worry about that side. The inside's just night passage, mostly U.S. ships out of Seattle so they don't have to deal with customs and everything when they hit Alaska. You'll only be out during the day, right?"

She nodded but scanned the list of boats and the times they should be traveling through the strait. There was something niggling in her brain, but she needed to look at the brochure more thoroughly if she was to understand whatever it was.

She got lucky when a fisherman came to launch his boat, taking Trevor away to deal with the transaction of launch fee and ensuring the boat was safely launched. In the meantime she shoved the ship schedule in her pocket and they launched their kayaks.

It was a good day to be out on the water. Blue skies, light wind, only a light ripple turning to chop in the center of the channel. The air was so clear she could pick out the individual trees on the islands, and the coastal mountains shone ghostly white. They struck out southward, Alice in the lead because Phoebe knew she owed the girl that—at least. As it was, her mind wasn't on the paddling; it was sorting through all the facts that she had.

A dead whale with its teeth removed. A dead kayaker who cared about that whale. Dead eagles. Other than being dead, what did those things have in common? The boy loved the whale according to his parents. And he had shown an interest in eagles enough to start to download articles and even websites.

So what did eagles and orcas have in common—aside from both living in Johnstone Strait—and dying there?

A lot like three teenagers in her classroom. They had all lived in Langley and had all died in their school. Other than that, the three of them had very little in common. The two students Rick had killed were both from middle class homes with both parents while Rick had a single mother who had been struggling financially.

She shivered at the lack of answers just as Alice gave a joyful cry.

She'd managed to paddle about fifty feet ahead of where Phoebe was and just when had that happened? She was turned out to the open water and pointing.

A constellation of three, five—no, make that eight—tall black fins carved through the water, their curved black backs like small, more solid waves through the rippling water. Without asking, Alice drove her paddle into the water and set out on a trajectory that should meet up with them.

Phoebe quit her pondering and lit out after her. The girl was quicker than she'd expected, actually widening her lead as she skimmed over the water. The pod kept coming, running through the light waves, then whoosh, one of them drove up out of the waves and slammed down on his side, a silver cascade of water sent barreling into the sky. Alice screamed in excitement as another whale rose skyward, then splashed down sideways. Then another. It was like the whales played for joy.

They were headed for the coast, likely for the rubbing rocks Mike had pointed out to them. They just needed to get ahead of the whales before they came in close to the rocks.

Alice kept madly paddling in front of her and she did, too, and gradually cut the angle with the whales so they fell behind her.

Were they still angling toward the shore or had they reconsidered? Mike had said that the pods usually circulated around the strait. If that was the case, then the whales could be right behind her.

A sound like the largest sigh in the world came from her left. She glanced back.

Whale fins as tall as she was were coming up behind her, dark smooth backs curving out of the water. She felt like squealing and shouting to the moon as they came around her. She wanted to just stop paddling and let them draw her along with them, but she kept paddling, didn't want to get left behind.

They still surged past her, the huge huffs of breath spraying her with water. One fin towered above the rest, a male, while the females sailed past him, a smaller youngster in their midst.

Ahead Alice had slowed, waiting for the pod to catch up to her. Phoebe kept paddling and looking into the water and wondered what she looked like to the whales looking up at her. Then Alice was beside her and they paddled along, the pod of orcas gradually pulling away from them. And then they were gone, following the coastline southward to Robson Bite. She and Alice had long since passed the spot where they should have crossed the strait for the islands. Instead, the coast they followed dimpled inward away from them, exposing the cove where they had stopped for lunch their first day paddling.

Today there was someone there.

Chapter 12

THE COVE WAS A GENTLE CRESCENT OF SAND backed by dark forest, with rocky outcrops at either end that lifted in jagged edges toward bluffs that looked out on the strait, but today the tide was out exposing the tidal pools that Alice had explored. There were also six people despoiling the lovely little beach. They were huddled around something at one end, a zodiac pulled up on the sand and a larger metal-hulled cabined boat anchored farther out in deeper water. It took Phoebe a moment before she realized the men were in uniforms, some green, some blue, and that the boat looked official, too.

Studying the scene, Phoebe back-paddled, bringing her kayak to a stop as Alice continued following the whales.

The men ashore had obviously found something beyond what Constable Burns had told her. The fact that they weren't police said this was more likely about the eagle band or the whale tooth Alice had found. She could alert them to what she had found across the strait on the island.

Alice coasted up to her side having come back from the whales. Her eyes still shone. "Wasn't that fantastic, Auntie Bee! It was even better than that day with the tour group because it was just you and me!"

Phoebe looked at her blankly, then realized she was talking about the whales. Somewhere, in seeing the men in the cove, all her delight at the whales had disappeared. She nodded, but looked back shoreward. "It was good, all right. Something I'll remember all my life."

"So… are we going to head over to the islands or what? Race ya!" Alice went to turn her kayak with some quick paddle-work.

Phoebe held up her hands against the splashing. "Hold on. Would you just hold on a moment?"

The splashing subsided and Phoebe shook her head. "Before we head to the islands, I need to talk to these men." She hooked her fist at the cove. "I'm sorry, Alice. I really am. But I need to do this."

Alice looked from the shore to her aunt and her look of frustration slowly dissolved into a cagey grin. "You're still investigating."

Phoebe shook her head. "No. I'm not. I just need to tell them about what I found on the island. It shouldn't take long. We'll get in and out and head for the islands." With that she struck out for the shore. There was splashing behind her as Alice turned her boat and came after her. Soon they were both nosing their boats toward the rocks of the tidal pools.

Easing the kayaks sideways into the rocks where they dropped off to deep water, she used her paddle to steady the boat, got her butt up and onto the hull behind the cockpit, and managed to get her feet onto the rocks without a tumble into the water. Alice, much spryer on her feet, was already up and waiting for her.

"Do we beach the boats?" Alice asked.

"How about you hold them for us for a few minutes. Like I said, this won't take too long."

In her paddling boots, she slipped-slid across the rocks toward the men on shore. They saw her coming and sent one of the men to meet her where she reached the beach. He wore green—Provincial Conservation Services.

"Sorry, ma'am. This beach is closed. There's an investigation underway." He was young—weren't they all?—barely in his thirties by the look of him. Tall, blond as a Nordic god, and with a summertime streak of gold across the front of his mop of hair that was cut short over the ears, but longer on top. He was leanly built, like a runner or perhaps a swimmer—certainly an outdoorsman.

"I understand that. That's why I'm here. I think I may have information to help in your investigation. This is about eagle parts, isn't it?"

His gaze flickered a little in surprise, but he was good at hiding it. "I'm sorry. I'm not at liberty to say." His gaze flickered to Alice and he frowned as if a twelve-year-old girl didn't quite compute with what he expected.

"That's my niece. We're not media or lookiloos." She fished in her pocket. "Yesterday we were out paddling around Hanson Island. We had lunch at one of the small islands at the south end. I went exploring and found what looked like a hidden camp. I found these." She pulled out the silver bands and handed them to him.

He looked at what she held out and then back to her face. Back to the bands. Her face.

"There were more. There were carcasses, too. I don't know how many because they were just skeletons, but at least a dozen. I left everything else as it was and got out of there."

He finally picked up one of the bands to examine.

"Chris!" he called, turning to the others who were still bent over something amid the sand and stone. "Chris, get over here. You need to hear this woman."

Chris turned out to be a grizzled veteran, also dressed in green. Of Aboriginal heritage, he had short black hair that had faded to grey, and the weathered lines on his face said he'd spent a lot of his life in the outdoors and seen too much. His eyes—almost black—suggested that maybe too much of it hadn't been good and at the moment they were dissecting her.

"I'm Senior Conservation Officer Chris Wilcox. What can I do for you, ma'am?"

"My name's Phoebe Clay. I was just telling your officer here that yesterday my niece and I were paddling the south end of Hanson Island. We had lunch on one of the little channel islands and I found these along with a bunch of eagle carcasses. None of them had feet." She held out the silver bands, the five of them gleaming too harshly, it seemed.

"Jesus," he swore under his breath and his face went hard.

He picked up one of the bands and examined it. "This explains why some of those nesting pairs disappeared. They'd been coming for years to the same crag."

He eyed Phoebe. "Why didn't you report it to the police?"

"Uh, would you believe I've seen a little too much of the police these past few days? My niece and I were there when the whale rolled up into Pirate Cove. We also had the misfortune to be with the kayaking tour that found that dead boy. We've been questioned by police left, right, and, center. I want to save my niece from more of that."

Chris glanced over her shoulder at Alice. He nodded. "I've a granddaughter about the same age."

Alice was picking up rocks in the tidal pools, the kayaks on their tethers dragging behind her.

"This is a poaching ring, isn't it? They want feathers and claws."

Chris nodded. "For traditional Indian dancers and inclusion in Indian art. I've even heard it said that it's the New Agers wanting feathers as they search for authenticity by taking on aspects of North American Indian cultures. But mostly I think it's the Sundance Circuit wanting their regalia. Back in 2006, they were saying that a single genuine wing feather could fetch a hundred and fifty dollars and a tail feather two hundred and fifty. Now—it's more in the thousands for a perfect tail feather because they are so rare."

He shook his head. "Dammit. I thought this stopped when they got those seven down by Squamish. Seven Aboriginal men shooting eagles. It makes me gag." His hand fisted over the silver bands and an angry light flared in his eyes.

"It looks like the poaching's just moved farther up the coast," the young blond officer said.

"How many birds?" Chris asked.

Phoebe shook her head. "I don't know. Twenty, maybe. A dozen at least."

Another oath from Chris and he stomped away back to the other men.

The youngster watched him go. "You'll have to pardon him. He'd pretty passionate about our work. He's from the Kwakiutl First Nation from around here. He was the first from his nation to get his master's degree and he did it studying eagle populations. Bald eagles can live thirty years so he got to know a lot of the birds out here. He's been looking at why the population had plummeted the last couple of years. We suspected there was some poaching because feathers with DNA from local birds were showing up in some contraband regalia, but nothing of this scale. Some feathers could turn up because they are supposed to come from birds that have died from natural causes. As a matter of fact, we hadn't been able to prove anything was happening at all because we couldn't find the bodies. Not until an eagle band was found here by a tourist." He stopped and glanced out at Alice. "Let me guess. That was you, too. I heard it was a girl who found it."

"Alice. It was Alice. She was beachcombing like now, while I was dozing. Funny. She said she didn't go near this end of the beach because there was a bad smell."

Blondie nodded. "That's the bodies. Ten of them."

Chris came stomping back with another of the men, this one in Fisheries and Oceans blue.

"She and her niece were the ones who found the initial eagle band," Blondie said.

"And the whale tooth," Phoebe said cautiously. "There's a connection, isn't there?"

"Just tell us your story. All of it, from the beginning. Miles, you take notes."

Miles, aka Blondie, fished a notebook and pen out of his shirt pocket and Phoebe sighed. "Okay. Any idea how long it will take?" She glanced over at Alice. "Thing is, I've already messed up my niece's vacation enough. We were headed over to the islands but I thought we'd best let you know what we found. We'd already be there except a whale pod caught up to us and we weren't going to cut short that experience."

Chris looked at her and then at Alice. "Tell you what: you and your niece give your statements and then we'll run you over to the islands." He checked his watch. "All goes well, we'll have you there before eleven, which is about when you'll get there paddling, even if you leave right away."

He was right. By her watch it was quarter to ten. It would take them at least an hour to cross the strait. "Just let me let Alice know."

Alice was, thankfully, agreeable, so the two of them were interviewed once more, Miles taking Alice aside and Phoebe facing

Chris and the Fisheries and Oceans officer. When she was done with her story of her few days in Pirate Cove, she felt exhausted.

Chris nodded Miles toward the zodiac and he herded Alice in that direction.

The aging conservation officer stopped her to thank her. "Thank you for being as observant as you are. You've really helped us. Miles and Jerry'll take you and your boats across to the islands. They can check out the camp you mentioned and then come back for us."

She nodded and was turning to leave when he caught her arm. "Be careful, Phoebe Clay. These poachers are nothing to trifle with. There's a lot of money at play—to them. From what we know, it's no longer a mom-and-pop operation. If it was, we'd have caught them already because getting the bird parts out of the country isn't that easy. If that kid that died stumbled upon them—well, you see what I'm saying?"

"You're telling me this is organized and that by coming here I could have put Alice in danger." Her stomach felt like a stone as she eased her arm free. Her gaze followed Miles and the slim blonde figure who was deeply engaged in conversation with him.

She swallowed. "I feel like I should wrap her in cotton batting and send her back to her mother. I've wanted to, but Alice keeps demanding to stay. I guess I'm going to have to be the big meanie and pull the plug myself."

Chris nodded. "It's hard to watch them grow up. Harder still to keep them safe."

She wanted to be sick. All those children who had been safely in her care didn't mean anything compared to the three she had failed. Didn't mean anything at all compared to keeping Alice safe.

"Thank you for your warning," she said. "I appreciate it."

They traveled out to the Fisheries and Oceans boat in the zodiac, their kayaks dragging behind them. At the boat, Miles and Jerry clambered up the stern and hauled the zodiac close to the side of the boat so that Alice could clamber up with Phoebe coming behind. Alice was like a little monkey swarming up the rear of the boat. Phoebe passed up the kayak ropes, which were tied off for the trip across the strait. Then she fought her way up onto the deck with Miles' help. When she was finally standing on the deck, Jerry started the engines and they started out with the two kayaks gently bumping the sides of the towed zodiac.

They came out of the cove into the strait where the wind had picked up and buffeted them. Alice retreated into the cabin with Jerry to help steer the boat and he dubbed her an honorary Fisheries and Oceans staff and placed a Fisheries baseball cap on her head.

Overhead, the sky was still clear blue. "Is it going to stay like this, weather-wise? Yesterday we went out and got in a squall heading back. We nearly got run over by a cruise ship, too. The darn thing didn't even slow down." Phoebe shook her head at Miles.

He nodded. "They seem fast when you're in a kayak, but really they're not that quick. Our zodiac can keep up with them—at least for a while."

They made it across in the boat in twenty minutes and pulled into the channel Phoebe and Alice had visited the day before. With Jerry holding the boat steady, Phoebe, Alice, and Miles slid down into the zodiac and he held their kayaks steady for each of them as they slid into their cockpits. In a quick leap, he was back up on the stern of the boat and waving goodbye.

"Alice, your hat!" Phoebe motioned at Jerry's cap and pushed her kayak up beside Alice, plucked the cap off her head, and paddled like mad after the boat. Jerry, thankfully, kept the boat at a steady pace and Miles was leaning down to grab the hat by the time she got the kayak up beside the boat and a little ahead so she could ship the paddle and hold the cap up. Miles grabbed it, tossed her a toothy grin, and Jerry sent the boat cruising around the island to the side where Phoebe had discovered the birds.

It was quarter to eleven and they were on the right side of the strait. The sky was blue; the water was, too—in places, the turquoise color of the tropics. The edges of the islands were littered with small bays that shimmered in the sun and they ran into the small family of otters again. They drifted, charmed, watching them, then carried on, but the whole time their situation ate at Phoebe.

She shouldn't chance Alice's involvement in whatever was going on—she just needed to figure out how to break it to her. Who knew Northern Vancouver Island was such a hotbed of intrigue and crime?

At one o'clock they pulled into a small beach silvered with the remains of old snail shells. It sat sheltered by three pillars of rock topped with lone fir trees that had been tortured out of shape by wind. The water of the bay was shallow enough that they waded out, chasing minnows as they went, then they settled on the beach and pulled out the coke and PB-and-J sandwiches they'd made for lunch.

"Can we come here tomorrow and spend more time?" Phoebe asked as she lay back on the sand, the sun catching her happy, closed-eyed grin.

Phoebe looked down at the happy girl. If she could only freeze-frame this moment—this wonderful, magical moment so the two of them would have it forever, no matter what happened and how much time passed.

She sighed. "That's something I wanted to talk to you about. I'm not sure we should come out here again. You remember those eagle bodies."

Alice's eyes were wide open now and she rolled up to sitting. "Yeah?"

Phoebe gazed out over the water. It was so peaceful here with the summer sun shining down and the clear blue water that it was hard to believe this was happening. But then, hadn't that been what school was like, too? A regular classroom except for the internal torment of one boy.

"They were poached, Alice. Like people in Africa poach elephants for their tusks. The eagles they killed for their feathers and their claws. You saw that printout of Alex's. Eagle feathers and claws are used in special dance ceremonies. The feathers are supposed to come from birds that die naturally, so the feathers are very expensive. I guess like with the elephants, somebody got the idea that they could just hurry the birds' deaths along. That's why you found that silver ring. The reason Miles and the other men were at the beach was that more birds had been found there, too."

She shifted to face Alice. "Chris, the man we met back in the cove, he said we need to be careful because these poachers are dangerous. I don't think your mom would want you out here if she'd heard his warning. I don't either. This is going to be our last day of paddling."

"But Aunt Bee! If we just stay on the beaches or out in the kayaks, won't we be okay?"

"I—I don't know. But we can't take that chance." She thought of Alex Parker. Had he come across the poachers? Was that why he'd died? He'd been an experienced kayaker, so it wasn't the accident the police had told the media. If he'd run afoul of the poachers, it would explain a lot. He'd been at the right place at the wrong time. Like two other young people who had tried to do the right thing.

A hallway scented of books, floor wax, and the sweat and pheromones of young bodies. In the too-bright fluorescent lights, bright posters celebrate the various school clubs from their spots on the walls between the classroom doors. And young Rick Hames stands alone with the gun in the hallway, threatening the kids who had made his sister's life hell. He'd plans to shoot them, but Judi Markus and Harb Sidhu, two of Rick's friends, leap in to try to stop him. Gun blasts and screams and those two young bodies fall and she—she is pushing students back into a classroom when Rick looks right into her eyes. Haunted. Terrified. Desperate.

She knew those eyes. She slams into the classroom, slams the door behind her. Locks it as another gunshot roars from the hall. She hears the thump of another body fall. All because no one would listen when she'd sounded the alarm about how Rick Hames was acting—not aggressively, but like he was withdrawing until the only person he hung around with was his younger sister Jennifer.

All because she hadn't done enough herself.

"You're thinking about Alex, aren't you?"

She jerked and shivered with the sudden need to vomit. A sudden gust of cold air found her bare legs and arms. She blinked and brought Alice into focus.

"Him. Other stuff. How what we see is only the surface of things." She tried for a smile but didn't quite make it and covered with a cough. Shook herself. "Tell you what, let's enjoy today and make our decision tonight. Okay?"

They spent the afternoon exploring the little bays hidden along the quiet interior channels between the islands, then turned for home and the Johnstone Strait crossing, but all the while her mind was churning. Rick on the floor in a pool of his own blood. Judi and Harb gone. And people had barely acknowledged how they'd failed Rick. No, it had been the lack of mental health services, lack of supervision by his parents, lack of programs. The fact his father had a gun that he kept locked in a gun safe, but Rick had learned the safe combination. But Phoebe knew where the fault lay—in her—in the fact that though he'd come to her for help stopping the bullies who were after his little sister, she hadn't gotten anyone to take action. The bullies had operated outside the school system.

And so she'd left him to take action. If only she'd taken the next step herself.

Had something like that happened to Alex? He was a loner just as Rick had been. But that didn't mean that he didn't yearn for friendship. That need for acceptance could make you do stupid things when you're young. What if he had been involved in the eagle poaching but he'd ended up in the poacher's bad books?

That thought ricocheted around in her head so that she was distracted as they headed out of the channel into Johnstone Strait.

"Aunt Bee, look!"

Another pod of whales coursed through the water not fifty feet from them and coming fast toward them. They rested their paddles across their cockpits and waited for the whales to come around them, but behind the whales, another boat was following. Big old cabin cruiser flying a big old Canadian flag off the stern. Three children were crowding the bow of the boat, another two were standing on the rear deck. The captain up on the pilot's deck was pushing to come in even closer to the whales.

"He's chasing them!" Alice said.

"The idiot is going to hit them if he's not careful." Phoebe grabbed her paddle and drove right through the oncoming whales toward the cruiser. Thankfully the boater had the good sense to turn away. "What the heck are you doing! Give them some space! You could have hit them just like you could have almost hit me!" And that could kill them just like Light Fin had died.

"There was a baby in that pod," Alice said coming up beside her.

"Probably why they were trying to get in close so those youngsters on the bow could see."

"Sometimes I don't think I like people very much," Alice sighed.

"Join the club, honey." Phoebe reached over and tousled Alice's hair.

Chapter 13

With the weather on their side, they made it back to Pirate Cove before four thirty. The sky was still deep blue and the water glimmered in the sun, but as the sun's angle shifted, the mountains of Vancouver Island placed the cove in shadow. Still, the bright white and yellow and green buildings around the harbor welcomed them home. The brick-red building that housed the Whale Interpretive Center, however, sat like a sullen blight on the picture.

The journey across the strait had been so quick and easy Phoebe and Alice could have stayed out on the water longer. Phoebe, however, had a few other things on her mind that she'd been chewing over. Eagles. This was all about the eagles, she was sure, and it felt kind of prophetic that an eagle was soaring high in the sky above the cove as they turned into the harbor. If it was all about eagles, she couldn't help but think about the eagle that had surprised them in the Whale Interpretive Center. Just what was the eagle doing there? The place had been filled with skeletons—not exactly the place you'd expect to find a living bird.

Could pleasant-spoken John Wilbur and that less-than-pleasant Meredith woman have something to do with the eagle parts trade? She should just go to the police with her suspicions, but she had learned long ago not to accuse somebody of something until you had proof. Nope, she needed to look into her suspicions herself. Then she'd go to the police.

They were coming into the boat launch when a zodiac spun past them heading out into the strait. The driver waved as he passed them by. Trevor, a fisherman's toque pulled down over his penny-bright hair. Beside him was Bert Clarke, the fisherman she'd spoken to that first morning by the whale. The zodiac's wake gave them a nice little push the final few feet into the concrete launch and they had to back-paddle to stop the kayak hulls from scraping on the bottom.

They climbed out and unloaded as Donnie came over to check the kayaks over.

"We're not sure we're going to be using the kayaks tomorrow. Would it be possible to make the decision in the morning?"

Donnie, freckle-faced and sunny-smiled as ever, just shrugged. "Shouldn't be a prob. The boats are right here. You don't take them, no skin off my nose. Trevor'll understand."

She nodded her thanks, then looked up as the kid was leading Alice's kayak along the water over to the storage area. "Say, the Whale Interpretive Center, does it have anything to do with live animals?"

The kid frowned. "They study whales, I guess. Least Doc Wilbur does." He shrugged.

"Do they do anything with other kinds of animals? Like maybe eagles?"

"Nah. It's a *whale* center. Not birds."

"Guess we'll have to check it out," she said and let him get on with his job.

"What was that all about?" Alice whispered to her as they carried their belongings up from the water.

"I was just thinking about that first night we came off the water. Remember the eagle?"

Alice's blue eyes widened. "And there was that rude lady." She looked thoughtful. "You know, Alex was really angry that morning."

"You mean at the whale being dead?"

"That, but it seemed to be other things, too. Like he was mad at somebody. He kept swearing under his breath—saying bastards over and over and over."

Phoebe frowned. "I don't remember any of that. Do you think he was mad at the professor?"

Alice shrugged. "How should I know?"

But no, she didn't think he was mad at John Wilbur because he'd actually sought out John when he found the whale. "Let's go find that professor and see what he says."

Alice shrugged again—an action that was becoming a rather infuriating habit and that said she was getting perilously close to moody teenagerhood.

They bundled their things into their day-packs as best they could and clumped down the boardwalk to the red-colored, warehouse-sized building. At least today they were earlier, and the pleasant weather meant the door to the interpretation center was open. From the afternoon sunlight, they stepped into the gloom. The skeletons gleamed whitely under their spotlights. The woman, Ayisha Meredith, stood behind the welcome counter, her dark hair once again pulled back in a severe ponytail. She looked up with a bright smile, but when she saw who it was, the smile faded.

Okay, for some reason the woman didn't like them.

She came around the counter to them after scanning the long hall of the center. There was no one else there. "Hi. I remember you. You were looking for Professor Wilbur the other day."

Her low, smoker's voice grated and Phoebe's stiffened, expecting another lecture. "Yes. We were. And you weren't too helpful in finding him if I recall."

The woman glanced down the room again. A figure had appeared from the back and was sweeping the floor. The woman stepped in closer.

"Listen, I'm really sorry about that, okay? You surprised me and after Light Fin—well, I was an emotional wreck. Please accept my apology. I'm not usually like that. I'm Ayisha Meredith, by the way." She stuck out her hand.

What the heck? "Uh—of course. I'm sure it was all a misunderstanding. I'm sorry we disturbed your bird. I'm Phoebe Clay and this is my niece Alice."

Surprised didn't quite capture the emotion Phoebe felt. She shook. Released and was pleased to see Ayisha introduce herself to Alice as well. So many adults forgot to.

"Nice to meet you both under better circumstances." Ayisha sighed and shook her head. "Darn eagle got out of his cage somehow and reinjured his leg. John found him floating out in the water last week. He's young—hasn't got his white head and tail feathers yet. I guess he'd been fishing and caught too big a salmon and couldn't lift off again once the weight of the fish pulled him into the water, so there he was, floating with his wings spread to stay afloat and try to reach land. Poor thing wasn't far from drowning. Anyway, John brought him in and we were just keeping him quiet in a dark room hoping the wound on his leg would heal. Then we'd let him go. Now, though—well, John's had to call Fish and Wildlife to pick him up and take him to a rehab center. They'll be here tomorrow."

Phoebe took the information in and decided to play along. "Do you get eagles in here often?"

Ayisha, certainly chattier than she'd been before, shook her head. "We're all about the water and the mammals that live in it." She started leading them down between the skeletons, explaining what they were looking at and where the bones came from. "Have you seen many orcas since you've been here?" she asked.

"Three pods up close," volunteered Alice, studying the skeleton of a porpoise. "And we saw some of these and otters, too."

"River otters, and we saw three groups of whales; whether they were different pods would require a more skilled eye than I have," Phoebe said. Well in for a penny... "I think we've actually seen more whales than eagles, now that I think of it. Isn't that strange?"

Ayisha frowned. "Actually, it is. I don't pay a lot of attention to the birds, but I always remember thinking how lucky we are up here with all of the eagles around. Where I'm from in California, we don't have anywhere near as many. Once I actually thought about focusing on them in my study—sort of the marine habits of the bald eagle, but something larger caught my eye." Her dark eyes gleamed in the dim room. "Orcas. Blackfish, as the First People call them. Now there's a species. Family groupings that stay together for generations, but all of the populations are under real pressure now. The ones here are probably doing better than most, but the crash of the salmon stock down south really hit the southern residents. That's why I chose to study here."

The woman was so open it was hard to suspect her of anything, but that didn't mean she didn't need to talk to John Wilbur. "Listen, I hate to ask, but is Professor Wilbur around? I had something I needed to talk to him about."

Ayisha frowned. "Hey, Trish! Is the doc still out back."

The figure sweeping in the shadows looked up. "Yeah. Why?"

"Phoebe here would like a word with him. How about you take her out back and I'll continue the tour with her niece?"

Alice nodded "please," so Phoebe followed her guide outside, only then recognizing the girl as her waitress from the restaurant.

"Hi. I believe we've met—almost. At the boat launch and at the café. It was good food." Well, she'd been pleasant before, she might as well be consistent. She stuck out her hand. "Phoebe."

The girl looked at her offered hand and back to her face before shaking her hand. "Trish Rayburn. Glad you liked the food."

Rayburn. The resort owner's daughter? Her tone still suggested she really didn't give a damn, but she led Phoebe out back to where a boat motor had been taken apart and spread on the ground over a blue tarp. Another tarp had been draped over a wooden frame and tied down to protect the parts from the weather. John Wilbur was busy fitting pieces of the motor together against a backdrop of tree-covered slopes, the water lapping the pilings underneath them. Trish turned and left.

"Professor Wilbur. Phoebe Clay. We met the other morning at the dead whale."

Wilbur looked up, his blond hair tangled and his hands blackened with grease. He looked from her to his hands and grinned.

"I remember. Guess I won't be shaking your hand. How's that niece of yours? You've survived your kayaking trip?" Then he frowned. "Sorry. I'm guessing you might have been in that group that found—Alex."

"You'd guess right, then."

He shook his head and got back to work, fiddling with the grease-blackened parts. "That must have been quite a shock. I heard one woman fell completely apart."

"That would be Myrna. And yes, it was. I've had worse shocks, though."

He met her gaze and must have seen something for he nodded. "Worst thing I ever saw was a person who'd been mauled by a shark. It was in Australia and the kid had been surfing. Shark came up under him and took his leg and his hip. He didn't stand a chance.

"So what can I do for you, Ms. Clay?" The thingamabob had gone where he put it and now he was trying to put the entire piece into a do-ma-hickey.

"Phoebe, please. I had a couple of questions that I hoped you might help me with. The first is a simple one. What killed Light Fin?"

He shook his head and kept working. "Internal injuries from a massive blow. A boat, most likely. Her ribs on her left side were crushed. It's likely she couldn't swim well so she should have drowned. Oddly, she didn't." He sighed and stopped working, his gaze on his hands. "The worst part? Those wounds on her mouth? They were done while she was alive."

The horror of it almost made her knees go weak, but she held herself upright.

"The poor animal." Phoebe bowed her head and swallowed back the bile threatening her throat. She couldn't think about the whale. Couldn't think about the pain because it brought memories of other senseless killings—the premature ending of other young lives.

"The second question—and I know this might seem strange, but it's about Alex." There. A safer topic, maybe. Her breath was coming in short little gasps that she fought to steady out.

John Wilbur looked up at her, a question in his gaze.

"He—he seemed like a really nice kid and I can't get his death out of my head. A bunch of things have happened to me and my niece since we got here and I wanted to ask—did Alex have any interest in eagles at all?"

Wilbur frowned and kept working. "Now that's an odd question. I'd always figured his primary interest was in orcas, but this summer when he came home from private school, it wasn't too long before he started to talk about eagles and population sustainability. I thought it was a result of a combination of him being a budding naturalist and because of our star boarder in the backroom—we've had an eagle convalescing. Are you saying there might be something more to it? 'Cause the police were asking about Alex, but I never mentioned that to them."

Phoebe shook her head, "No," though she had a sense things were starting to fall into place. "I just wondered is all."

At that John Wilbur set down his grease-covered parts and set his hands on his hips. "Ms. Clay, you cannot come in here and ask me about Alex and eagles without telling me why."

She found a grim smile at his consternation. "Actually, given it would be premature for me to be casting suspicions to the wind, I believe I can. And I'm going to, I'm afraid. Thank you for your time, Professor." She nodded, shifted her day-pack on her shoulder, and headed back out to find Alice, the afternoon suddenly streaked with darkness around her.

They carried their gear back to the cabin, Alice chattering on about how Ayisha Meredith was actually really nice and how the bears come right down to the ocean to fish in the water and how that meant that they should be really careful when they sat on the beach to have their lunch.

Phoebe listened and nodded in the right places, but when they got back to the cabin, she sent Alice for her shower, sagged into a chair, and pulled out a paper and pencil to start to an inventory of what she knew.

A dead whale that should have drowned and had been mutilated while she was alive. She couldn't imagine any living animal standing for that. A dead boy. A dead, very smart boy, who was a loner and who had a love of whales. He'd also over the past three months taken an unusual interest in eagles that totally surprised those who knew him.

Kids didn't diverge from a learning trajectory so suddenly without something pushing them. And could it be coincidence alone that would push a kid into researching eagle sustainability at exactly the same time that eagles were being poached all around him?

She didn't like what she was thinking. Alex had been involved in the poaching. At least the paper his parents had given her with the Native regalia website suggested he could have been. If the police had taken the other articles he'd pulled as evidence, they had to be pursuing that area of investigation.

Then why hadn't they questioned John Wilbur about it? Did they suspect the professor was involved in some way?

It didn't make sense for a kid who was so clearly upset over the death of a whale and who was so clearly an environmentalist to suddenly become a rabid poacher of another protected species unless there was some pretty powerful motivation. In her experience with students, there were only two things that motivated the kids she'd worked with. One was money and status. The other was love.

The Parkers seemed well enough off and Alex had his scholarship to the very best of schools, so money didn't seem like the motivator, unless there was something about Alex she didn't know. Another thing to ask the Parkers, if she had a chance to speak to them. That and whether he had a girlfriend.

And then there was Alice's bit of information about how Alex had been swearing that first morning. "Bastards" could just be him swearing at whatever boat had hit Light Fin, but it could also have been him swearing at the whale's condition. The loss of her teeth. Phoebe shivered off another bout of revulsion and remembered the furious expression on Alex's face standing over Light Fin that morning. To do that to a *living* animal. Whoever had done it was—she couldn't find a bad enough word for them.

Alice came out of the bathroom in a gust of sweet soap-scented steam just as Phoebe was turning her mind to who might be involved in the eagle poaching. Alice was rosy-skinned, her long hair combed straight and still dark with water. From her paddling shorts and t-shirt, she'd changed into her jeans and long sleeved shirt and fleece, for it got cool here in the afternoon with the wind off the water.

Phoebe slipped her notes into her pocket and stood. "Do you want some hot chocolate while I have my shower?"

"Nah. I think I'll read a little bit." She pulled out her smart phone. "If I want hot chocolate, I'll make it."

Phoebe was about to protest when she recognized the competence on Alice's face. She was growing up before her aunt's eyes. It left her feeling old and physically tired after the day of paddling and the emotional turmoil of whether to stay or leave Pirate Cove. If she left now, she knew she'd never come back because the place would always have the same kind of dark miasma about it that had kept her from returning to work. If she stayed the extra day and went paddling, she would be putting Alice at risk. She wasn't going to do that.

Alice looked up from where she'd sprawled on the couch and was scrolling through something on her smart phone. "You having that shower? Cause I'm getting hungry and I know you don't approve of pre-dinner foraging."

"God, you can be old at times!" Chuckling, she left for the bathroom.

Chapter 14

THIRTY MINUTES LATER, SHOWERED AND dressed in clean clothes, she and Alice left the cabin into the late afternoon sunlight. Through the trees along the hillside path, the sun had disappeared so they trooped down a trail with gloom fading in under the trees around them. There were still plenty of birds though. Thrushes with their red-V'd chests. Flickers with their bright cheek patches flashing as they peck-peck-pecked at the tree trunks for bugs. The croak and long, quiet soar of a raven overhead. Life was still up there, closer to the light, but at the moment, Phoebe felt like Light Fin must have felt as she sank down into dark water.

Just when she'd hoped this trip with Alice would help her find the surface again.

"You're really quiet," Alice said as they came out from the trees near the Parker's blue house. Phoebe looked at the place, almost hoping the Parkers would see her and wave her over, because she wasn't going to lead Alice to that place again. Nope, the kid deserved at least one halfway normal day—well, evening at least.

"Sorry. Just a lot to think about. We still need to decide whether we're going to paddle tomorrow or call it a trip today.

Today was a pretty hard act to follow once we got over to the islands. It might be nice to leave with those memories."

"But I don't want to go. I want to go paddling out to the islands on a nice day and paddle around."

"But didn't we do that today?"

Alice rolled her eyes. "No. We spent half the morning talking to those Fisheries guys."

"Fisheries and Conservation. You liked them. You got to run the boat that took us over to the island."

Alice screwed up her face. "Okay. That was fun, but we still didn't spend all day paddling. We haven't done that—ever."

"But we did on day one together, remember?"

"Nu-uh. There was the whale, remember?" We didn't get out onto the water until late."

The kid was going to hold that against her, too. They pushed into the restaurant still arguing like a couple of high school best friends. The place was quiet, only a couple of the locals Phoebe recognized. Bert from that first morning by the whale. Donnie, his son, was with him. It was probably one of the few times father and son had together given how busy Sam Rayburn seemed to keep them. Nice that they made the time to eat together.

They both nodded in her direction and she raised a hand in response; she led Alice to a table on the far side of the restaurant. She didn't want to disturb them with what could become a heated debate when it came to finally making a decision.

Trish, the waitress, pushed out of the kitchen, saw them, and brought them menus and water. She was wearing the ubiquitous Pirate's Cove red polo shirt with jeans.

"Hi," Phoebe said. "By the way, thanks for taking me back to talk to John Wilbur today."

The girl shrugged, told them the soup of the day was black pea and lentil, and walked away.

"Boy, she doesn't get any better, does she?" Phoebe said.

"She's rude, Mom would say," Alice said with wisdom beyond her years.

"Maybe she just has other things on her mind. Now what appeals to you tonight, Ms. Alice? Your wish is my command as long as there are vegetables involved."

"Aunt Bee!" spoken with a perfect teenager whine. "But I want a hamburger."

"You've had burgers for three nights in the last four." Pick your battles, woman. You have other battles to win tonight—like getting Alice out of here. "You can have your burger, but there has to be a salad or green vegetables on the side, too. Eaten, I might add. And just so you know, you have officially perfected the whine of someone at least three years older. Your mother will be so proud."

"My whine? Mom said I had that perfected last year." Alice gave a toothy, satisfied grin. "Okay. Cheeseburger and fries with salad on the side with Thousand Island dressing. Please."

If only all battles were so easy.

Behind them the restaurant door pushed open and the reporter, Mina, and a young man Phoebe recognized as her cameraman entered. Heart sinking, Phoebe turned back to Alice. So much for a nice relaxing dinner with Alice, even if they were going to debate the merits of staying or leaving. She nodded at Mina, dreading the grilling that was going to come. The brunette smiled back, but she left her companion and headed in Phoebe's direction.

Good God, not that, too. Phoebe kept her head down in hopes that Mina would pass them by for the women's washroom. Didn't work—Mina stopped right beside them. Alice looked up, forcing Phoebe to do the same. The woman's well-known dark gaze was waiting.

Mina held up a hand. "Before you say anything, Phoebe, let me have my say. I'm not here to interview you. I just wanted to apologize to you. The media was hard on you back then." Mina looked at her hands. "I know you did your very best. That's all I wanted to say." She nodded and retreated to their table in the corner. It was a peace offering—a sign that she wasn't trying to intrude. Okay. At least that was something.

Trish came back and took their order, then pushed into the kitchen, letting the door swing behind her. It allowed a view of the kitchen like the one they'd had their first night when Phoebe had caught a glimpse of Alex back there. At the time she'd thought he probably worked here. Had he?

When the food came, Trish tried to drop their plates on the table and run.

"Excuse me." Phoebe stopped her. "Could I ask you a couple of questions?"

"I'm working, can't you see?" the girl turned to go.

"It's about Alex Parker. Did he work here?"

The girl seemed to freeze, then, "No," she answered and bolted for the kitchen door.

What the heck? It was a simple enough question. The answer shouldn't get her that upset—unless…

"Alice, honey, I'm going to go have a word with our waitress. You wait right here, okay?"

Alice nodded and stared out the window at the water. The light was failing and taking with it the colors of the harbor. The last charter boats were crowding the entrance to the cove, chugging in with the last stray sunlight catching in their windshields. Then the light was gone and the scene grayed through the window. Phoebe left her and pushed through the kitchen door.

A hot fug of grease and grilled meat was stirred by air streaming in an open rear door that gave out toward the water. The room was long and narrow, with brushed steel counters down both sides, a steaming deep fryer and meat sizzling on the grill on one side. Two plates stood on the counter beside the grill, hamburger buns complete with all the fixings except the meat and fries. Her order. A burly cook stood by the grill, but Trish was slumped just inside the door.

"Hey! You can't come in here," she said.

She'd been leaning on the counter as if she was shaken. When Phoebe entered, Trish scrubbed her eyes. She shoved her dark ponytail back over one shoulder as if that would help her get back in control.

"Please. Go back to your table." She pointed at the door.

"I need to talk to you and if you won't talk out there, we'll talk in here."

The girl's mouth firmed in a line and she tried to shove Phoebe toward the door. Phoebe pushed back. *God, what was she doing? Weren't there health laws or something about the public in a cooking area?*

Phoebe held up a hand. "Look, I'm looking into what's going on here in the cove. There's been too much happening: Light Fin's death. Alex's death. The mutilation of the whale. Other stuff. Alex was here the first night we ate here. It looked like he was upset about something. If he didn't work here, why was he here?"

The girl turned away. The cook, a big bruiser of a guy, eyed Phoebe. He didn't look that friendly. He nursed the two hamburger patties frying on the grill. He had a full head of frizzled red hair and piercing blue eyes that seemed to take them in with barely disguised disgust.

"Frank, would you take a break or something? I'll turn the burgers, but I need some privacy here," Trish said.

Frank shrugged and left and the girl went to stand guard over the hamburger patties. "Alex was here because of me. He was my—friend, all right?"

Friend or boyfriend?

"But there was something going on that night. Neither of you were happy."

"We had a fight. People do." She flipped the burgers and for a moment the sizzle of meat filled the room.

"What were you fighting about, Trish?"

The girl glanced up at her, then busied herself placing two slices of cheese on each of the burgers. "None of your business. It was personal."

Phoebe looked her up and down. The mousey girl played tough, but at the moment it came off more as mouse-nervous. So maybe the whole toughness thing was a sham. She decided to take a chance, just as the girl slid one of the burgers on a bun and turned for the other. "Was it about the eagles?"

Trish dropped the burger cheese-side down on the grill. The stink of burned cheese filled the room and she scrambled to right the burger.

"Shit, shit, shit." She got it upright on the bun, but the damage had been done—half the cheese left behind, bubbling on the hot surface. She rounded on Phoebe. "See what you made me do? Those are your burgers."

Phoebe shrugged. "You haven't answered me yet."

The girl's face seemed to crumple and she sagged her hip against the grill, covering her face with her hands. "Oh God, don't you realize what you're doing? This is fucking unsafe, lady."

"What d'you mean, unsafe?" The echo of Chris's words chilled her skin and all the other sounds dropped away as she focused in.

The girl was weeping, swiping at her eyes as if she was mad at them, too. "Look what happened to Alex. It could happen to you."

"Are you threatening me?" The heat of the grill went freezer cold and she remembered that feeling. It was the sensation she got when dealing with danger. The sensation you got pushing a hall full of kids into a classroom and slamming the door before a gun went off again.

"No." The girl hung her head and her shoulders seemed to collapse as she sighed. "No. I'm scared. Terrified they might come for me, because I knew Alex. I wanted him to get out so bad, but he wanted the money. He said he was going to help me get out of here—away from my dad. He owns the Pirate's Cove and everything in it. When Alex wouldn't quit, I told him I'd refuse the money. When he left he said he was going to talk to my dad." She turned haunted brown eyes toward Phoebe. Funny how the kids who looked the toughest could crumble the fastest.

But the fear in Trish's gaze was real. "Please, please get out of here. Please leave me alone. Just take your niece and get out of this town. Please. I'll cook you new burgers and wrap them up. You can take them back to your cabin and leave in the morning. Please."

But Phoebe was so close to understanding that she had to know. "So what was Alex trying to protect you from, Trish? What was so important that Alex would do something so far out of what he normally would do?"

"It's none of your business, like I said."

She'd tossed two new patties on the grill, and readied fries for the fryer. Phoebe wasn't about to accept her silence. She walked up to Trish and pulled her around to face her. "What's going on with you, Trish? What would make Alex willing to risk everything to help you?"

The girl felt limp in Phoebe's hands, all of her resistance melted away. Trish looked up with huge brown eyes that pleaded for help, at the same time as they begged Phoebe to go.

"My dad. He's like a trap I can't get loose from. Did you ever see a wild animal caught in a leg-hold trap? They'd chew their leg off to get free. Dad—he loves me—but he won't let me have a life. He's going to keep me here in Pirate Cove for the rest of my life." The tears were coming now—huge gushers flowing down her cheeks. "When Alex got his scholarship, there were actually two given out. I won one, too. But dad wouldn't let me accept it. He said he needed me here to help in the Cove. It's a family business and that should be what we all focus on. He told me I wasn't good enough for that school." She hung her head. "I believed him, until Alex started sending me copies of assignments from the school and I could do them. He even handed one in as his own and it got an A—just to prove to me that I could do it. I told my dad to show him I could do the work and he went ballistic. I swear he was looking to kill Alex..."

"And now Alex's dead."

The transformation from anger to abject fear was as catching as the plague. The fact the girl's words echoed the warning of the Conservation Officer just seemed to close up Phoebe's chest. Sam the resort owner, or the eagle poacher. Either could be responsible for Alex's death. She couldn't breathe. Couldn't breathe and she found herself backing toward the door, suddenly very, very afraid of everyone in Pirate's Cove. She turned and slammed through to the restaurant seeking something normal, gasping for clean air free of kitchen grease and the miasma of fear.

She looked toward the table that had held Donnie and Bert. Not there, but a bundle of bills lay on the table. She turned toward her table and did a double take.

Alice wasn't there.

Chapter 15

The restaurant ached around Phoebe, the empty table and chair like the empty desk in a classroom when a student dies. Only the reporter and her cameraman at their table in the corner. The scent of hot grease and burned cheese stung her nose and amped her desperation for air.

"Alice?" Her voice seemed to echo. She had to be here. In the washroom maybe? That was all it was. She should stop her panicking.

She plunged down the hallway that led to the washrooms, shoved inside, the door banging against the metal towel dispenser. Sink. Toilet stall—empty. She whirled around and out the door and into the men's washroom in case Alice had made a mistake.

No Alice. "Alice! Come on! You're scaring me, honey." Her voice shook in her chest. Hell, it shook as her words hung in the air.

She ran back into the main room and Mina stood up from her table.

"Ms. Clay? What's the matter?" she asked.

Phoebe grabbed her arm. "My niece. Have you seen her? Where did she go?"

Mina looked confused for a moment, but then her face cleared. "I wasn't really paying attention. She got up and went to the washroom, but when she came back the young man from the other table came over. They were talking and your niece seemed to know him, so when they left together I didn't think anything of it."

"Alice wouldn't do that. She wouldn't. She knew I was concerned about everything that was happening." She whirled around and slammed back into the kitchen just as Trish was pushing out the door with two dinner plates. The plates smashed to the floor. Phoebe grabbed Trish by the collar of her now-food-spattered, red Pirate Cove polo shirt. "Where is she? Have you seen her? Alice?"

"Jeeze!" Trish shoved her away, all her attitude back in place. "What's wrong with you, lady?"

Beyond her, the burly cook was back at his spot by the grill.

"My niece. She'd gone. Have either of you seen her? I told her to wait for me while I talked to you." Oh, God. Oh, God, it was all happening again. The world was coming apart.

"Well, maybe you shouldn't have left her waiting so long!" Trish said.

Without thinking, Phoebe slapped her, leaving a vivid red brand on the girl's cheek. The trouble was, it was true. Too true. Alice had been upset when Phoebe had questioned the Parkers. Had she overheard her talking to Trish and left? Got tired of waiting and gone back to the cabin in disgust? Phoebe turned tail and ran.

Out of the kitchen, out of the restaurant. While she was inside, darkness had seeped into the cove and she was blind when she stepped out of the restaurant. Felt blind, too. Alice. She had to find her. If anything happened to her…

"Probably nothing's happened to her. She just went home," Mina had followed her outside and looked at her kindly.

But she'd had that kind of wishful thinking before, hadn't she? *The denial that nightmares can't happen, and yet they could. They had. She had lived through one of them.*

And others had died.

"Oh, God." She ran. Down the street past the blue house to the trail up through the forest. Plunged into the greater darkness and stumbled on. Tripped and fell to her knees in a thick stand of sword fern before she fished out her flashlight and then sprinted up the hill.

The cabin looked like they had left it: normal. The porch light they'd left on gleamed over the cabin door. A single light left on inside placed an amber glow on the windows. Normal. She was here. Had to be here. She reached the door and tried the knob. Still locked.

"Alice. I'm sorry, okay? Alice, let me in and we'll try this again. Alice, please." Damn it, she was sobbing as she fumbled her key into the lock and pushed the door open. Please let those big blue eyes be waiting. Please let her be pissed off and cheeky and a normal twelve-year-old with a tangled mop of blonde hair.

The door yawned open and the scent of shower steam and this morning's hot chocolate wafted out to her. No one on the couch. No one on the bed. "Alice?" She rushed over to the bathroom—empty, of course.

The room went cold. Okay. She'd let herself panic, now it was time to get herself under control. That was how she'd kept the other kids calm in an impossible situation. Stay calm. She'd done it then, she could do it now. She fished her phone out of her pocket, sank down on a kitchen chair, and dialed Alice's number.

The call tone burred into her ear. Again. Again. Again. Until it flipped over to voice mail.

"Hi!" Alice's bright, happy voice came over the phone. "I'm not here for your call because I'm having an adventure with whales. Leave a message. Please." The "please" an almost afterthought and she could imaging Becca standing over her, reminding her of the magic word.

Oh, God, Becca! How could she tell her sister she'd lost her baby?

There was no way. Becca would die. Becca would look at her the way those parents had at the funerals.

Damn it, what was she doing? She had to find Alice. She leapt up and looked at the phone in her hands. Stabbed 9-1-1.

"9-1-1 Emergency. Police, fire, or paramedic?"

"Police."

'What is your emergency?" said the police dispatcher, but the slowness of the damned woman's voice had her vibrating where she stood.

"My niece is missing. She's only twelve. I—we're in Pirate Cove—or I am. She just disappeared from the cafe we were in. I've searched the restaurant and I've checked our cabin. She's not there. She's not anywhere." She could hear the panic she was feeling creep into her voice.

"Slow down, ma'am. Can I get your name?"

"Phoebe. Phoebe Clay. Constable Burns—she knows me and my niece. She questioned us about the dead whale and the death of the Parker boy. Please—I think this is about the eagles. I think they've taken Alice because they knew I was getting close to solving the case."

"Ma'am, I don't know what you're talking about. Now what's your niece's name?"

"Alice. Alice Clay-Standish. She's visiting from Ontario."

"Are you her guardian?"

Guardian? It was so hard to think. "Not legally, no, but I have letters of permission from both her mother and her father. They're divorced."

"Did you have a fight with your niece, ma'am?"

A fight? A fight? "No. Yes. Maybe. I don't know. I wanted her to consider leaving Pirate's Cove because I didn't think it was safe here. She didn't want to go. We went to dinner to discuss it and now she'd gone." All the fear bubbled up again.

"How old is your niece, ma'am?" So clinical and cold.

"I told you. She's twelve. Only twelve. She'd blonde with blue eyes. About five-feet-six. She was wearing jeans and a pink hoodie over a blue Hello Kitty t-shirt." She closed her eyes to stop from crying. "Listen. Could you let Constable Burns know this has happened? Tell her I think it has to do with the whale and Alex Parker and the eagles."

"Ma'am, how long has your niece been missing?"

She checked her watch. "Twenty minutes now, I guess. She was just in the restaurant and someone said they saw her talking to Donnie and Bert Clarke. Now she's gone."

"Ma'am, that's not very long. Have you talked to the Clarkes? She's probably still with them. I'm sure she's just upset and has gone out for a walk with friends."

Phoebe looked at the phone, her entire body gone cold as if the deep water of Johnstone Strait had just filled her bones.

"You listen here, young woman. Alice would not do that. We had an agreement that she was not going to do anything I didn't tell her was safe and I told her to stay put. We did not have a fight of enough significance for her to leave. Donnie and Bert Clarke are not friends. They're barely acquaintances. She is a responsible twelve-year-old and she knew how worried I was about her safety. She also was well aware of the terrible things that have happened here. She would not leave on her own. I am sure of it. Now you either pass this along to Constable Burns or someone else with the power to help me, or I'll have your name and will be talking to your supervisor."

"Hold for a moment, please."

She felt like she was vibrating with the need to do. To act. To be anything but the person that helplessness was overwhelming like deep water.

Her phone beeped in her ear indicating an incoming call. She checked the number.

Alice!

She accepted the call, cutting off the dispatcher. Didn't matter. Alice was found.

"Alice! Where are you, honey? You had me worried sick!" She could shout for joy. She'd lecture the girl later.

"She's with me. Frankly, she doesn't seem to be doing that well," a strange male voice spoke from the other end of the phone.

The cabin disappeared around her, the walls, the furnishings turning to mist and she was back in a fluorescent hallway, a gun coming up in a young hand and she was shouting, "Rick, no! Stop!" but the muzzle was already flashing and she could feel the impact of the words just like bullets into her own heart. She swallowed back the iron taste of fear.

"Bert? Is that you?" She thought maybe it was, by the voice. "Where are you? What have you done to her? If you've hurt her, I'll kill you."

She would, too. Somehow. She hadn't been able to save Rick or Judi or Harb, but she was ready this time. She had swallowed her fear so many times in her dreams that this time it didn't hurt so much to breathe. She could do this.

"What do you want?"

"I *wanted* you to get your big nose out of my business. Now I figure we need to have a talk to see if your little blonde niece is going to get out of here at all."

"I don't believe you've got Alice. You could just have her phone."

A terrified squeal came over the phone, and then, "Aunty Bee?"

"Alice! Honey!"

"I'm okay, Aunt Bee. We just ruined these guys' schedule."

The phone was ripped away and the male voice came back on. "You'll get your ass down to the launch. There'll be a kayak waiting. Get out on the water and we'll call you and tell you where you're going. Call the police and you'll never see Alice again. Don't try anything. We'll be watching."

The call clicked off and she stood there frozen, inhaling the dusty scent of the cabin. The phone vibrated in her hands and she looked down. The RCMP calling back. Constable Burns, perhaps? Or the dispatcher. Take the call?

She'd rolled her eyes too many times at the television shows where the family member refused to seek the help of professionals. The trouble was, in her experience, the professionals had never been that helpful in dealing with the situation. In the case of Rick Hames, she'd alerted administration and the police that she was worried that he might do something stupid. The kid hadn't been bullied himself, but he hadn't been able to deal with the bullying his sister was experiencing. As Rick had become more withdrawn, anxious, and his attitude darker, she'd expressed her concern to the powers that be, but they didn't believe that he would do anything as permanent to try to deal with the situation. She'd asked for counseling for Rick and for someone to take action against the kids bullying Jennifer, but until Jennifer or Rick actually came forward to make a complaint, it wasn't going to happen. They expected the matter to be dealt with through general anti-bullying education and awareness programs. So no one *did* anything. Or at least they hadn't until Rick had taken matters into his own hands and done something in the hallway at school.

She should have done more. She should have walked Rick down to the principal's office. Should have, could have, would have—if she hadn't thought she'd done enough. She had to do more to save Alice. But should she try, once more, to go through channels? The phone buzzed two more times.

She stabbed the accept call button.

"You listen to me. I just received a phone call from Alice's phone. It was a man saying they had Alice and they were going to hurt her unless I came to them. If I called the police they would kill her. I don't know where they are, but I have instructions to take a kayak out on the water. They'll notify me of where I'm going then. If you can help me, fine. If not—well, I'm going."

She stabbed the phone off, but not before she heard Sarah Burns yelling at her to stop. Too bad. So sad. Alice was somewhere and she was feeling bad. Phoebe was out to cure that.

She pulled off her jeans and pulled on a pair of shorts, grabbed her paddling boots and her waterproof jacket, and then ran out of the cabin. Night smothered the landscape; the few lights of Pirate Cove were only symbols of man's futile attempts to hold back the darkness. What people forgot was the darkness existed inside themselves. They carried it with them into the brightest sunlight—or into fluorescent hallways.

She stumbled down the trail, following her flashlight and praying that they hadn't hurt Alice. The wind in the treetops sounded like a woman moaning, or maybe she was, she couldn't tell. The only thing that mattered was getting to the water and out to wherever they had her sunny little girl. Her sister's baby. She remembered flying back to Ottawa soon after the birth and holding that small bundle of life in her arms. The way those blue eyes had looked at her in trust. They'd never lost that trust, but they had to have today. She couldn't let that happen. She had to live up to that trust. Succeed, where she'd failed Rick.

The town was closed up tight, the restaurant dark as she ran past, but down the road a flashlight bobbed. The kidnappers keeping tabs on her? She rushed past. She should never have cornered Trish like that. Or maybe she should have pushed harder. She hadn't gotten the names of the eagle poachers.

The harbor was quiet. The tide was in, water lapping deep and murky under the boardwalk, a light swell rocking the moored boats. The tink-tink-tink of sailboat mast hardware grated like the scree-scree-scree of a horror movie. Overhead, wind-scuttled clouds blew across a crescent moon that reflected off the waves beyond the harbor. There were whitecaps out there. Not any place she wanted to paddle.

She ran down the boat ramp, found the blue kayak she had used that day beached just above the water, and glanced around. Donnie? Or Trevor? God, could they both be in on it?

"We just ruined these guys' schedule." Alice's words came back to her. It was an odd thing for anyone to say. Odder still for a twelve-year-old. Unless she was trying to tell Phoebe something.

Alice was smart. Smarter than most kids her age when it came to working things out for herself. She was trying to give Phoebe a clue. The only schedule they'd come up against in the time they'd been here had been the schedule they'd gotten from Trevor. Was Alice trying to tell her that Trevor was involved? Or was there something else about the schedule of cruise ships traveling through Johnstone Strait waters?

She had to let the police know.

She was dragging the kayak to the water when a Gore-Tex-clad figure stepped out of the darkness.

"Phoebe? Have you found her? I've been looking around the Boardwalk, but I didn't see her." Mina stood there, flashlight in her hand, her dark hair damp from the ocean air. The lights from the harbor caught in her cheekbones and jaw so that she looked like something out of a Rembrandt painting.

Phoebe shook her head and kept dragging. If Alice's abductors were watching, she didn't dare tell this woman anything.

"Has someone contacted you?" Mina asked, coming up to her as Phoebe pulled on the spray skirt so it hung off of her by its suspenders.

She looked up and met the woman's gaze, willing the reporter to understand.

Mina went still. Then she backed a pace. "They have and they're watching. Things'll go bad if you say anything."

Phoebe blinked her agreement. Mina might be media, but she was here and she was offering to help. Phoebe kept working on the kayak, slid into the cockpit, but not before she let the cruise ship schedule drop out of her pocket. She nudged it with her foot as she splashed into the water and climbed into the cockpit. A last glance at what she'd dropped and then she started paddling. Please let the reporter be as smart as she seemed. Please let her contact the police and share the information.

She drove the kayak away from the shore without the spray skirt in place, and she wished she'd remembered paddling gloves. It was cold and getting colder just in the cove. The wind had turned from the north, coming down from Alaska and the Bering Sea. It was going to be worse in the full cold of the strait.

She paddled out from the shore and pulled her phone from her pocket and held it in her mouth as she fought with the spray skirt. When she finished, she hit Alice's number on speed dial. It rang once, twice, and then came the click of pick-up as she rode the waves.

"Hello Ms. Clay. I was about to make your niece pay for breaking your promise."

Panic struck at Phoebe's heart. "Promise? What promise?"

"You were not to talk to anyone, yet you had a helper at the boat launch."

"No! Listen to me. The woman—she followed me. I didn't speak to her at all. If you were watching, you know." God, had they seen her drop the schedule? Her little signals?

"Not good enough, Ms. Clay. Listen."

He must have held the phone away because suddenly there came a squeal of pain that could only be Alice.

"Alice! No! You bastards! What have you done to her?"

"She'll survive. For now. Consider it a warning not to try anything else. Now I hope you're ready for a hard paddle. You know the channel between the islands you've gone through the past few days? You're to head out to the middle of the strait between that channel and the cove on the mainland. We'll contact you there to give you the next coordinates. My watch says that it is eighteen minutes after nine. I'm giving you exactly thirty minutes to get into position…"

"Thirty minutes! There's just no way! I've been paddling all day."

"Then I suggest you quit protesting and get to paddling if you want to see little Alice again."

The line went dead and Phoebe's heart pound against the walls of her chest so fast she could barely breathe. No time to call the police. Just paddle.

She shoved the phone in a baggie and thrust it into her bra, then dug in her left blade and started.

Chapter 16

As soon as she left the cove, Phoebe was fighting for her life—for two lives. The wind tore at her hair so it whipped her cheeks. It wasn't raining, but the salt spray and spume off the waves were almost blinding. The only light came from the young moon and the clouds that ripped across its face. The water was a black maelstrom that came from all sides. Just how was she supposed to make out the island well enough to get into position? Even if she was sure where she was going?

All she could do was paddle and pray that between here and there she'd figure out a way to get both her and Alice out of danger. They sure as heck weren't luring her out there out of any concern for her welfare.

At first she stuck close to shore because she thought she could make better progress where the cliffs might give some modicum of shelter. She quickly realized that wasn't going to work. It was taking too long and her most precious commodity was time. She drove the kayak out into the water. Unfortunately she'd traveled far enough south that to aim for the channel she had to take about a ninety degree angle to the coast and that meant she was traveling almost broadside to the waves. They sluiced over her boat and her spray skirt, almost rolling her. If not for the spray skirt, the little craft would be swamped. The wind and waves roared.

No way in hell was she going to survive if she kept on like this. She had to take a chance and aim slightly more into the waves. The wind caught her body like a sail and push her along, but she had to be careful, because it was going to be the trip from hell to paddle into the wind to get into position if she went too far south. She prayed Mina would contact the police with the information and would get it to Burns or to someone who could help her.

She drove in her paddle, her shoulders beginning to burn. She didn't know how long she'd been out here because she couldn't see her watch. Paddle, just paddle. She checked over her shoulder for the channel between the islands where she and Alice had paddled. Dammit, she'd gone too far south and she was nowhere near the center of the strait. She had to try harder.

She turned the kayak, almost tipping herself again as the waves broadsided her, but then kept paddling. This time she was headed northeast, almost into the wind.

Alice was everything. Alice needed her help just as desperately as Rick's sister had. Tormented and alone, with no one to help but Rick. She could almost understand what had led him to bring that gun to school. Not senseless at all. She understood his motive—could understand him all too well because if she had a weapon, she'd use it, regardless of all the horrible things that could result.

Adrenaline burned through her as the wind howled in her ears. She should have seen that she was getting too close to understanding their secret and that this would be a threat to Alice. She should have seen that her innocent conversation with Rick to take action about Jennifer could lead to what had happened. It had seemed so simple, said with such good intentions. She'd meant that Rick should go to the authorities with the facts of what was happening to his sister. He knew directly. They would listen to him, when they hadn't to her. But Rick had chosen to interpret her suggestion differently. She should have walked with him down to the office. She could have. Should have, would have, could have. But it had been easier to give him the night to think it over. It was the end of the school day and she had been tired.

She squinted against the stinging salt spray. Well, she might be tired now, but she was doing the right thing.

Adrenaline pinged in her veins and she sent the kayak surging forward through the roaring night. Almost there. The channel was coming up on her right. *I'm coming, Alice.* If Alice was here, she had to be in a boat. She scanned the waves but there was nothing to see. No running lights. She glanced over her shoulders. No— *holy shit!*

Southward, the night was alight with a huge white ship, gold lettering on the bow announcing it was the Tropical Queen. The ship cruised directly at her and she realized part of the roar in the darkness wasn't the wind but the giant workings of massive marine engines. She had to get out of here!

Paddling into the waves would just leave her in the huge ship's path—a scenario she had to believe had been the intent of the voice on the phone. But this had to be what Alice was referring to. The ship. Was she sending a warning along with a call for help?

She turned away, toward the islands, and almost rolled the kayak when a wave hit her broadside. Kept going and brought the craft around to face the behemoth threatening her. The waves were behind her now, the sea alight with the ship's growing reflection. She plunged her paddle into the water, letting the wind help her as she drove across the waves. The wind pushed her and she angled toward the islands out of the huge ship's path. She hoped. She prayed.

Paddle. Just paddle. Her blades churned the water, but she was a dragonfly against a semi-truck and about to be flattened against its windshield. No one would see her in the darkness because a kayak didn't have running lights. Who would expect a kayak to be out in such a night? If the massive ship caught her, she'd be cut in two. Even if she was just close, there was a good chance she'd be swamped or drawn under, down into the darkness and the maelstrom of the huge ship's propellers. There'd be barely enough left for any searchers to find. The remains of an idiot tourist gone insane, finally, after her breakdown after the school shooting. When they'd found her and the class, she'd been sitting there crying, the students crowded behind her, but she hadn't been able to stop, had she? She'd ended up hospitalized, and even when she and the doctors had said she was well, one step into a school and the panic had started again and so had the waterworks. And now that insane woman had dragged her poor, unsuspecting niece out into a crazy night of paddling. A niece who would never be found—like the missing girls? The thought almost froze her.

The huge ship's bow towered above her, sending its wave against her. Too close. She had to be farther away. Alice. Damn it. Was this mad paddle just to get rid of a meddlesome woman while they dealt with Alice someplace else?

"No, damn you! I'm coming for you!" She sent the kayak surging southeastward toward the islands as the huge ship came even with her. The bow wave picked up the kayak and lifted her further away as the drum of the engine shook her through to her bones and all she could do was keep on paddling and ride the huge wave to stay alive.

And then it was past, the massive ship's turbines roaring through the night, the massive screws churning the water, and its lights showing a momentary trail of peace between its wake. Above the waterline, halfway up to the empty passenger railing on the stern, a door was open in the hull exposing a crew passageway. She turned into the wake trail and turned the kayak back northward. She's passed the channel in her mad dash for escape.

She'd escaped. She had.

Where was Alice? Somewhere in Pirate Cove, being spirited away? Already thirty minutes or more down the highway to a new personal hell, like one of the girls who had disappeared?

Something dark surged out of the channel between the islands toward the cruise ship. A zodiac, low to the water without running lights. It barreled across the choppy water and came into the quiet trail behind the ship, then seemed to pick up speed to fall in behind the cruise ship. On the stern of the ship, two men appeared in the open crew passageway half way up the rear of the ship. They threw down a line.

The harsh light from the cruise ship illuminated what was happening. The following zodiac was quick and maneuverable on the waves. The people on the smaller boat maneuvered in close enough they could catch the line tossed down from the ship. They attached something to it and waved.

The men on the cruise ship began to haul in the line. A limp body cleared the deck of the zodiac and hung suspended, limp and silhouetted against the ship's white hull.

Good God, Alice! This was how they planned to steal her away!

She paddled like a mad woman, even as the cruise ship and the zodiac pulled away from her. So far the zodiac had kept up to the cruise ship, but there was no way in hell she could catch them. The quiet wake was dissipating around her. She had to phone the police again and tell them what was happening. This was how they did it. This was about more than eagle feathers. This was how they got the eagle parts out of the country without going through customs. This was how the missing girls disappeared so completely. While everyone had been thinking serial killer, it was really a case of abduction. There *was* a lucrative international sex trade for underage girls.

Hadn't she read somewhere that cruise lines were now the greatest fear for terrorists getting into North America? Security at cruise ship terminals was never as stringent as at airports. In this case, they could drug the girl. A seasick girl going through customs wasn't going to get much attention.

She unzipped her jacket and fished for her phone. Stabbed 9-1-1 again and fought to get the spray skirt on while steadying the boat. The cruise ship was churning away, the zodiac still at the stern, sending up another load. Another limp person lifted into the cold fluorescent light of the ship.

"9-1-1."

"This is Phoebe Clay. I'm out in the middle of the strait…"

"Hold on. I'm transferring you."

A click and the white boat was disappearing away from her. She had to catch up. She had to get Alice. She looked at the phone in her hands. Looked at her paddle. Had to keep going. Had to reach Alice.

"Phoebe! Sarah Burns here. I've got you on speaker phone. Where are you?"

The clear voice of the constable cut through her panic and she could breathe. Could think. She swallowed back the black fear. "I'm in the center of the channel. I've just watched the Tropical Queen cruise ship go by. A zodiac has just met with the ship at the rear and offloaded two packages to two crew members. Two bodies. One is my niece, I'm pretty sure." She kept her voice factual when she felt like screaming.

"Hold on." There was a noise from the phone as Sarah obviously had a conversation. But the ship was fading away in the distance. The darkness closing around her like curtains and she was shrinking away, Alice was shrinking away into the light, just like in a horror movie.

Then suddenly the night northward was bathed with light. Two spotlights illuminated the huge liner. Another well-lit boat surged toward it as the waves closed in around Phoebe.

"We've stopped the ship, Phoebe. We'll find her."

Phoebe dropped the phone and started paddling northward into the waves, the wind, the light.

They found Phoebe forty-five minutes later, a charter fishing vessel commandeered by the police coming alongside her. At first she refused to acknowledge them. Kept paddling because Alice was that way. Was somewhere there in the cold, cold distant light ahead. She had to get her and pull her back. Get her back for Becca. Get her back to safety.

"Phoebe! Phoebe Clay! We have her! We've got Alice, or the Port Hardy police do. She's safe. Alice is safe!"

It was only the last bit said over a distorting loudspeaker that she finally understood. Her neck was stiff from strain and cold as she finally turned to look at the boat alongside. A man in uniform. Police. Beside him another man she recognized. Miles, the young conservation officer.

She couldn't seem to ship her paddle, just dropped her fists and the paddle onto the top of her cockpit. The waves instantly buffeted her, but the charter boat came alongside. Someone leaned down and caught the line on her boat. Someone else caught her by her shoulders and lifted her up, clean out of the kayak, and dragged her aboard, the paddle still firmly in her hands. She collapsed on the deck and they had to help her pry her fingers off the paddle.

"I have to get to Alice."

They wrapped blankets around her and pulled her up. She couldn't feel her legs, but she stumbled inside the cabin. They handed her a drink but her hands wouldn't work. Miles caught her shoulders and held something hot to her lips.

"Careful. It's hot."

Tea. Black. With milk and lots of sugar.

"I couldn't reach her in time. I couldn't get to her." Tremors ran through her and she felt like she was falling apart.

"But we did, Phoebe. We did. Because of you. She's in the hospital in Port Hardy. We're going to take you there, too."

With his help, she sipped more tea, but the shaking didn't stop. She sat there with the young man's arm around her shoulders and the waves of the world crashing around the boat's hull.

"You did good, Phoebe. You did real good."

It was a litany she didn't know whether to believe.

She started talking, telling him everything.

Chapter 17

PHOEBE WOKE TO THE ANTISEPTIC SCENT OF HOSPITAL rubbing alcohol and the sounds of people moving and voices over a loudspeaker. She lay curled on her side like a comma and the shoulder under her throbbed, but when she tried to move, every inch of her body screamed in protest. Even her hair seemed to ache and certainly her face did where her hair touched her cheek and forehead. She finally rolled over and moaned at the pain; tried to lift her hands to her face, but shifting her arms just wasn't going to work. Or it would only if she could stand the pain.

She opened her eyes and her vision cleared to reveal a white hospital ceiling and Becca's face hovering over her. She frowned, trying to think how that could be possible. It was just last night that the paramedics had met their boat at the Pirate Cove harbor and whisked her away to the hospital. She'd seen Alice then, still unconscious from the drugs the bad guys had given her, but safe and, according to the doctors, likely to have a full recovery.

Phoebe they had had to fight into an examination room. The diagnosis had been hypothermia and exhaustion and she'd continued to fight until they agreed that she could stay with Alice.

She'd tried to stay awake, to stay on guard, and had refused all the sedatives the doctors had recommended, but sometime in the night her exhaustion had gotten the better of her.

"Where's Alice? How is she?" She struggled to sit up, but her darned body just wasn't cooperating and she collapsed back on the bed.

"She's just out getting me a cup of coffee and herself a hot chocolate from the machine. How are you doing?" Becca's voice was full of concern. No sign of anger at how her older sister had nearly lost her daughter.

She was a pretty woman, ten years Phoebe's junior, with all the grace of the model she could have been in her fine-boned form. Her ash-blonde hair hung in soft waves around her face and somehow made her look another ten years younger. Her large blue eyes carried the vestiges of worry—clearing now.

"I'm fine, but I'm wondering how the heck you got here so fast. How the heck did you get to Port Hardy in the space of twenty-four hours?"

Becca smiled and dug under Phoebe's covers for one of her hands. Warm fingers twined Phoebe's and squeezed.

"Easy. I didn't. You've been asleep for forty hours straight. It's been two days since you chased that cruise ship through the dark." She shook her head. "From what the police said, by the time they caught up to you, you'd almost caught up to where they had the ship stopped."

Phoebe closed her eyes and remembered the dark and the dogged determination that she was not going to lose Alice. No, she wasn't going to lose anyone again. "I think I remember them fishing me out of the water, but that's about it. Until I saw Alice. She looked so small and vulnerable in the hospital bed that I almost lost it."

"They said you started crying."

Oh, God, not that.

"And then you stopped and smiled at everyone with the most beatific smile. And then, once you'd made them promise that you could stay with Alice and were in her room, you passed out. So they called me and here I am. I hopped the very first plane and got here yesterday afternoon. Alice and I stayed at the cabin last night. A cute little place, that."

Phoebe frowned. Her sense of time must be messed up. She didn't think she'd gone to sleep so quickly last night. She didn't think she'd slept so long, either. She shuddered at what she remembered of last—no that horrible night two days ago. If she'd started crying, she was surprised she'd actually stopped.

A motion at the door brought her head around. Alice stood in the doorway, two cups in her hands. Her eyes widened and she almost dropped them but for her mother's taking them from her, and then she had her arms around Phoebe and squeezed so tight it was almost more than Phoebe could handle.

"You're awake! Oh, Aunt Bee, are you all right? I was so scared when they said I had to just let you sleep!"

Phoebe buried her face in the scent of young girl, inhaled and felt her chest tighten. Oh, God, she'd almost lost her. She looked up at Becca, who nodded. She'd almost lost her for both of them. Her chest constricted, but she was not going to cry. She'd cried before, but this was a happy ending.

Alice pulled back. "I brought hot chocolate. Do you want some? You can have mine if you like and I'll go get some more. Don't worry. The vending machine's just across the hall and besides. Did you know? They caught the guys that were taking the girls who disappeared, all because of you!"

It was almost too much coming at her at once. "I'd like some chocolate very much, please."

Alice carefully transferred one paper cup from her mother's hand to Phoebe and then disappeared out the door again.

"She's busy acting very grown up after everything," Becca said.

Phoebe sighed and sipped the cocoa. Definitely not as good as homemade, but it was better than the iron taste in her mouth.

"Has she talked about what happened?"

Becca nodded. "Non-stop. More than I want to hear, probably. And lots about how her Aunt Bee figured it all out and got help. She describes you as very smart and very brave."

Becca raised her brows because they both knew that was stretching the truth more than a little.

Sipping her tea, Becca settled in the chair beside the bed. "The police said they'd be in as soon as they're notified you're awake and, given the fuss Alice is making, the nurses are probably aware of the change in your state. So why don't we take advantage of this little interlude and talk?"

Meeting her sister's gaze, Phoebe braced herself. She had a pretty good idea what was going to be said. She deserved the recriminations for dragging Alice into such danger. The blame for Alice's trauma. She held up her hand before Becca could start.

"Just so you know, I'll understand whatever you have to say. You have every right to be angry."

A puzzled look took over Becca's face, but two uniformed officers came to the door and knocked before she could say anything. She stood up. "You okay?"

Phoebe nodded.

"To do this?"

Another nod, though her body ached like nobody's business and she had the greatest urge to close her eyes again.

"Then I guess I'd best leave you in peace to deal with this." Becca turned to the officers, Sarah Burns looking her usual stern self and another officer, this one with stripes on his jacket cuffs and little clusters on his collar. "You be good to her and let her rest when she's tired, okay?"

"Promise," Sarah said.

"And see you keep it, because Phoebe is the nice sister." Becca tossed a wink in Phoebe's direction and the hallway echoed with the sound of Becca collecting her daughter before departing.

The eminently normal sounds of Becca's instruction and Alice's almost instinctive protest made Phoebe smile. Then she turned her attention to the RCMP officers. "So what can I do for you? Do I apologize now for all the trouble I've caused?"

"How are you feeling?" Sarah asked. "You know, you gave us all quite a scare when we couldn't find you out on the water. We had six boats out looking and it was only by accident we found you. One of the boats was heading back to harbor to refuel and came across you way out in open water. We thought you'd have headed for shore."

Phoebe closed her eyes and put her head back, suddenly exhausted. "Not when Alice was missing. Not when I didn't know if she was safe."

"But I told you we had her. Over the phone, remember?"

Phoebe frowned, seeking the memory, but all that was there was cold wind and colder water blowing in her face. Darkness all around and a distant light. Alice. Her almost daughter. She had to make sure she was safe.

"All I remember is the ship so far ahead. I had to catch up. I had to make things right." This time. She swallowed back the memories of when she'd failed.

She opened her eyes. "So what happened that night? I wasn't even sure that you got my message."

Sarah glanced at the other officer. "Phoebe, this is Inspector David Brindle. He's head of Port Hardy detachment. I'll let him answer your questions."

He was a tall man, clad in a dress uniform. He had sandy brown hair cut short over the ears, but with enough length on top to reinforce the appearance of youth around his eyes. This was a young man, destined for greater things for the RCMP to have given him his own detachment at this young age—maybe thirty-five.

He stuck out his hand. "Very pleased to meet you Ms. Clay. You are a very brave woman."

She managed to lift her arm up a little. "Sorry. I think I might have overdone the paddling." She grinned. "So just how did you rally enough forces to do what you did? I can't imagine it's easy to get a cruise ship stopped on short notice. They have schedules to keep and it was a US vessel."

He didn't shake her hand so much as squeeze it and set it gently down on the covers again.

"Actually, Ms. Clay, your call came in when we already had a significant investigation into the missing girls under way. That was running out of Comox detachment on behalf of the North Island. Locally we had a fair-sized joint investigation underway about the eagles with police and Conservation. We'd also brought in Fisheries and Oceans when the whale was found, but the two investigations weren't talking to each other. After all, it wasn't exactly obvious that the two fit together. When your call got passed to us that evening, we figured you might have broken the poaching case wide open, but your missing niece upped the stakes considerably and got the two investigations talking. That got us more resources almost immediately. Your friend, Mina, called in the information about the cruise lines connection and that brought in the big guns from Canadian Security Intelligence and the US's Homeland Security, and suddenly we had the ability to stop a cruise ship. So we found your niece and also caught the ring.

"We arrested three crew members on the ship. They had a nice little hidey-hole set up on the ship for their female guests. Near as we can tell, they were shipped, drugged, back to Seattle, where they could be transported wherever their captors wanted. Let's face it, they wouldn't have to pass customs because they were Americans and they could just be assisting a child that was sick due to seasickness. The girl would be gone and no one would be the wiser. Child traffickers used to be able to do something similar through the airports until International Customs and Immigration got wise. The cruise ship lines are our latest vulnerability. That'll be tightening up soon."

"So that's what this was about? Human trafficking? Let me guess—the birds were simply an off-shoot business and the whale teeth were just an offshoot of that."

"A bit more than that. The eagle poaching predates the missing girls, actually. We think the first girl to go missing might have stumbled upon what was happening much like you did and so they took her. It would explain why there was a longer period between her disappearance and the series of other girls. Once they realized they could do it, they had to set up a system."

She thought about that and felt the shaking start again. "So if we hadn't stopped the ship, Alice would have been sold into white slavery along with the other girl."

He nodded. "They already had another girl ready to go—a runaway they picked up heading down from Sointula to Vancouver."

"I saw them lifting someone onto the ship twice…"

"Your niece and the other girl."

She felt sick, it had been so close. She closed her eyes. "Who would do that—sell a child?" God, her eyes were so heavy.

"It surprised the hell out of us, actually, but catching them in the act loosened quite a few tongues. It was all run out of Pirate Cove. Sam Rayburn, the owner of the resort, ran into some financial problems with the economic downturn a few years back. The eagle poaching was a way to make ends meet and it kept them limping along. Then the girls came along and they were in business."

Phoebe nodded, taking it all in. "And Alex and Light Fin were afterthoughts, weren't they. Alex became involved with the eagle poaching trying to raise some money to help Sam Rayburn's daughter, Trish. But then he realized that poaching was reaching unsustainable levels and they were going to wipe out the resident population. He started to push back. Then the accident with Light Fin happened—at least I'm betting it was an accident. Probably when they were doing the transfer to the cruise ship or something. Alex was always out with the whales. He could have seen it happen. He could have seen them transferring girls, too. He even could have tried to help Light Fin. Leastwise she ended up in the little cove. Maybe Alex was going to try to get her help—that, we'll never know. But between him finding her and her washing up in Pirate's Cove, Sam's men found her, too. Maybe they didn't realize she was still alive or maybe they didn't care. They took her teeth and then they dragged her back into the water to finish dying.

Unfortunately for them, the tide brought her body into the harbor. I'm betting Alex confronted his compatriots and that cost him his life."

It was so similar to Rick she had to swallow back tears. A youth who tried to do the right thing—Rick trying not to rise to the bullies, Alex trying to help Trish. Both took action in the only way they knew how and both paid the price.

"What about Bert and Donnie Clarke? Were they involved?"

Inspector Brindle nodded again. "Those two were in it up to their necks. Donnie's a good looking young fella. He could pick up the girls without any problem and bring them in to his dad's place for warehousing until transport. We found eagle talons at their place and some very good scopes that would be perfect for shooting the birds. Bert wasn't talking, but Donnie talked. He called the eagle slaughter just a little harvest. After all, there were usually more birds to fill in where they took what they wanted. Typical attitude of some people that whatever's out there is there for the taking. Apparently Bert used to have a fishing boat but he lost everything in the salmon collapse. He wanted to buy himself a charter boat and get out from under Sam Rayburn."

She opened her eyes to look at the two officers. "That's a lot to take in. Thank you for being where you were needed and for saving Alice. I never could have lived with myself if something had happened to her."

As it was, she nearly hadn't. Following that light in the darkness, she'd known her strength was almost gone, but she'd had to keep going. It was the only way—the only way to redeem herself for the time when she didn't do everything she could have.

"I think we'll leave you to get some sleep. Constable Burns will be back to take your statement later this afternoon."

She nodded. "One more thing—was Trevor involved, or was it just a happy accident that he had that schedule?"

"As far as we've sorted so far, no, he wasn't. Sam Rayburn seems to have kept his own kids out of it, but things could change as the investigation continues."

Phoebe hoped she was right about Trevor—that he was a good lad. Her eyes closed before she even saw the inspector and constable leave.

Chapter 18

In the early morning shadows, mist clung to the surrounding tall cedars and hemlock that encroached on the pot-holed, dirt track that led toward the water's edge of Johnstone Strait just north of Pirate's Cove. Phoebe's trusty Subaru jounced along the rough surface, early sunlight through the trees momentarily blinding her again and again when a beam of light caught her full in the eyes. Beside her sat Becca, her long blonde hair pulled back in a ponytail, wearing Gore Tex and fleece against the cool air off the water. In the back seat, subdued, Alice curled in the corner, her mass of blonde hair tangled around sleepy, half-mast eyes. Darn kid *would* stay up late, but she had still gotten herself up at the crack of the crow to do this—pay their last respects to a young man they had barely known.

The dirt road dwindled and disappeared at the edge of the trees where low brush and mossy rocks made up a broad bluff that overlooked a small cove. Four other vehicles had beaten them to the spot: a pickup with 'Whale Research Center' emblazoned on the side, an RCMP suburban, a Toyota pickup with canopy, and a small Ford hatchback.

The occupants had spilled out onto the bluff, like four small shoals of fish that would not coalesce. John Wilbur and Ayisha Meredith stood beside their vehicle bobbing on their heels and talking as a brisk wind caught their hair. They wore the blue Gore-Tex jackets with the Research Center logo. Beside the RCMP vehicle stood Sarah Burns, in full uniform with the gold stripe running up the side of her navy trousers. She stared out at the water as if she was thinking. Beside the Toyota stood Hugh and Mary Parker looking somber in dark jackets, still an island of grief that no one was quite sure how to approach.

The fourth vehicle, the hatchback, sat off by itself, next to it two young figures stood alone by the bluff. Trevor Rayburn and his sister, Trish, Trevor's arm around his sister's shoulders.

"You're sure you want to do this?" Phoebe asked. "It's looking a little tense here—sort of Mexican stand-offish—like no one wants to face anyone else."

Becca shook her head. "They're all here for the same reason as us—to see Alex off and maybe to celebrate the things he did right in his life. 'Course if you don't want me here, I can stay in the car."

Phoebe glanced over to the backseat and Alice. "What about you, kiddo? Sleep or do this? Your choice."

Alice roused herself and shoved her hair back from her eyes. "Do this, of course. It's the right thing to do."

And there she was again—almost a teenager and one Phoebe could admire.

"All right. Then we'll do it together. Come on."

She pulled the Subaru in next to the Whale Research Station truck and climbed out of the car into the scent of brine and cedar. A stiff wind off the ocean mussed her short hair and cut through the fleece jacket she wore. Out on the water, the early charter boats were cutting through the gleaming waves, headed to the quiet channels out amid the islands, their paying passengers hoping for a record-weight salmon. The islands were low, dark green humps like a patchwork on the water and beyond them rose the white peaks of the coastal mountains as if they were the columns that held up the blue bowl of sky.

John Wilbur and Ayisha Meredith greeted them, Alice and Becca flanking Phoebe as she shook John and Ayisha's hands.

"Sad it has to be this that brings you back to Pirate's Cove, but it's good to see you again," Ayisha said and smiled in Alice's direction.

"This is my sister, Becca. She's Alice's mom." Phoebe did the introductions and as a group they gradually shifted over to join Sarah Burns.

She straightened when she saw Phoebe and smiled. There was none of the guarded reserve Phoebe expected from the woman. Instead Sarah gave her and Alice a hug.

"I didn't know you'd be coming, but I guess I should have figured. It's the kind of thing you'd do. I was just thinking about that night and about the crazy fool woman who was going to chase down a cruise ship in a kayak. It's good to see you well."

"It's good to be well, too. Becca and Alice have been staying with me the past month while I sorted out what I going to do. The good thing is that I realized I can't go back to school. I've decided to retire and not just because the school administration was telling me to. I've decided I'm going to go traveling. See the world and all that. Maybe figure things out and find some peace along the way."

"Sounds like the kind of adventure that would appeal to you," Sarah said.

"Tell that to Becca. She's still worried I'll fall off the earth or something." Phoebe nudged Becca with her elbow.

Becca looked heavenward. "If you were the kind of person who would just go lay on a beach somewhere I wouldn't worry at all. But my stomach clenches because you're the kind of person who does things like you did here."

"Sorry, sis. That's just something you are going to have to get used to. Of course, maybe you and Alice can come join me sometimes, depending where I am. You can keep me out of trouble—or we can get in trouble together, just like when we were kids." Phoebe grinned winningly up at her younger, taller sister.

Becca met Sarah's gaze with a "what can you do" shake of her head.

"It looks like they're starting," John Wilbur said and everyone turned to where the Parkers had retrieved a silver urn from their car. Together they carried the urn to the cliff edge.

Phoebe and the others joined them with quiet murmurs of condolence. Phoebe caught Mary's thin, artist's hands. The woman had aged, her blonde hair gone grayer, her attractive features gone wan.

"I just want you to know how sorry I am all this happened. Alex was a good kid who died because he tried to do the right thing."

Mary's clear blue eyes looked faded as she nodded. "I appreciate you saying that. There are others who aren't so kind, given Alex was mixed up in the whole eagle thing."

"Because he was trying to help someone. Just remember that. I do. So does Alice and this is her mother Becca. We all remember."

Mary squeezed her hand. "Thank you. And thank you for coming. I didn't expect it."

"Funny. I did."

Hugh held the silver urn up so that it caught the early rays of the sun rising above the distant mountains. Beyond him, farther along the edge of the bluff the slight figure of Trish in a plaid mackinaw shirt jacket seemed to stagger until Trevor put his arm around her for support.

Hugh lifted the top off the urn, and the wind lifted a puff of ash on the wind. "I'm sorry son. I'm sorry I wasn't there to help you when you needed it most."

A sentiment Phoebe knew all too well and the old iron taste of grief filled her mouth.

Hugh took a fistful of ash and held it up for the wind, perhaps a last desperate effort to connect with his son. The gray ash slipped through his fingers and was gone as if it had never been. His face clenched and he brought the urn down and turned to Mary, his eyes full, pain etched livid on his face.

"I can't. I just can't toss my boy to the wind. It isn't fair. A father shouldn't have to do this. It hurts too much."

And if Phoebe's experience was any indication, it always would.

Mary looked at the urn Hugh offered her and backed away. "You know I can't. I said I can't."

She swallowed, swallowed again and looked in Phoebe's direction. "Will you do it for us?"

Becca's hand clamped on Phoebe's arm in warning, but she pulled loose. There was no way that she wanted to do this. Not and carry another memory with her like a curse.

"Mary, don't you think that this should be done by someone who loved him? I didn't know Alex and Alice barely met him, but there is someone else who loved him and who is mourning him."

She raised her chin at the Rayburn siblings still keeping a respectful distance. They couldn't have had it easy since their father's crimes had come to light. The fact they stood apart spoke volumes about how the community was treating them and she understood how they must feel, too. She had walked their road, had nearly walked Hugh and Mary Parker's road too, but for the grace of God saving Alice.

The Parkers stood like statues against the glistening sea, then Mary seemed to breathe again. She took the urn from Hugh's stiff hands and led them down the bluff to Trish and Trevor.

"You share our loss," she said to the softly sobbing girl. "Maybe it would help you to release Alex to the place he loved the most." Mary nodded at the sea and swallowed again. "Would you do that for us?"

Trish wiped her eyes and looked up at her brother.

"You should do it, Trish. Alex would want you to."

Still sniffling, she nodded and accepted the urn. Together, she and Mary and Hugh turned toward the water. Trish removed the lid from the urn and turned it over into the wind.

Soft gray ash spilled into the morning. Some poured down the bluff face to the pebbled cove and blue water below. Some lifted up and blew over the bluff and still more seemed to suck out over the water on a breath of wind.

"Goodbye, Alex! Goodbye! I loved you!" Trish's cry carried out onto the water, Mary mouthing the words with her. Phoebe felt them in her heart—the letting go. The hope that the pain would eventually go away.

She caught Alice's and Becca's hands and tugged them back from the tearful group on the bluff. This was the time they needed to be with other people who knew Alex, who loved him and cared for him and had memories to enjoy. He was not and never would be her person. Not like these two.

"Come on. Let's leave them to their memories and go make our own."

Together they slipped away to the Subaru and toward home.

About the Author

Author of the well-regarded Cartographer Universe fantasy series, K. L. Abrahamson writes short fiction, fantasy, romance and mystery novels, as well as non-fiction for newspapers and magazines. Her mystery short fiction has appeared in anthologies such as Fiction River: Crime, and The Playground of Lost Toys. This is her first mystery novel.

A born wanderer, she currently lives in the Metro Vancouver area of Canada with two Bengal cats who channel James Dean's attitude. When she isn't writing she can be found with a camera and backpack in fabulous locations around the world.

To learn more about her, visit her website at www.karen-labrahamson.com and sign up for her newsletter to receive information on new publications.

To find more of her writing, visit www.twistedrootpublishing.com.

Also by Karen L. Abrahamson

Mystery
(Written as K.L. Abrahamson):
Phoebe Clay Mysteries
Through Deep Water

The Detektiv Kazakov Mysteries
After Yekaterina
Mareson's Arrow
The Tsarina's Mask
Ivan's Wolf

Aung And Yamin Mysteries
Death by Effigy
Death in Passing
Death in Umber

Fantasy:
The Cartographer Universe (in chronological order)
The Warden of Power

The Cartographer's Daughter

The American Geological Survey Series:
Afterburn
Aftershock
Aftermath
Afterimage

Terra Incognita
Terra Infirma
Terra Nueva

Sneak Preview- Shadow Play

When star investigative reporter Kaitlin 'Seattle' Blackwood arrives in Cambodia to look for her missing father, she drops right into the middle of the mystery her father left behind. A murdered monk, stolen rubies and missing orphans, all might be linked to her father's disappearance. So might B.J. McCallum the one man Kaitlin hoped never to see again.

Prologue

March, Phnom Penh, Cambodia

Jeremy Blackwood shook his head, ran his hands through his thinning hair, and tried to look calm and collected in the cushioned wicker chair at the bar's glass-covered wicker table. He sat just off the main street of Sisowath Quay, watching the mists off the Tonle Sap River turn yellow in the long line of haloed and pulsing streetlights along the road. They could lead you on like a young man's hopes. Or an old man's.

Beneath the lights, in the sweltering heat and next to the French colonial buildings, ran the seething mass of taxis, moto-taxis, motorcycles, and cars that belched out carbon monoxide and noise. It was the perfect bedlam for this grimy strip of real estate that housed the tourist bars and guest houses, and the dissolute expat community of Phnom Penh.

Which meant it wasn't so much mist around the streetlights as air pollution.

Time to stop looking at the world through shit-tinted glasses, old boy. After all these years, things were going to change—had changed—or would once the paperwork got signed at the Ministry of Lands.

He pulled his precious canvas satchel close beside him on the table, checking the flow of people along the boulevard. Nothing to worry about. Once the paperwork was signed, he'd be gone—at least long enough to prove to Kaitlin she'd never have to work again.

In this part of the street, upriver from the crenellated golden walls of the Royal Palace and the faded glory of the Foreign Correspondents' Club, he'd left behind the well-heeled tour groups. Here, the cheapo independent tourists filled the run-down, open-air restaurants with the rowdy sounds of drinking; surrounded by shifting halos of begging orphans, working girls, touts, and taxi drivers waiting for the tourists the drinks knocked down. It made him feel old. He'd given up drinking-for-the-sake-of-drinking a while ago. All it did was keep him from focusing on what he had to do.

But he was enjoying a drink here in the hole-in-the-wall restaurant just far enough off Sisowath that the crowds looking for entertainment rarely showed.

It was what Jeremy needed, after his years up-country. He'd spent enough time in the mountains to get used to the quiet, and Phnom Penh was anything but quiet. The city rumbled like an earthquake about to happen. It was almost too much—people—noise—entertainment.

He sipped his celebratory wine and frowned at the acrid taste—Cambodia was no place for wine. Not that Kaitlin would approve of him drinking anything. Again.

But the wine was red, rich with tannins. Not bad, given Pol Pot and his gang had destroyed pretty much everything French during their reign of terror. So civilization—if you could call it that—was just coming back to the city.

And soon he would enjoy the good life. He closed his eyes and let himself sink into the wicker chair's cushion, thinking about the new life he could finance for himself, his wife, and his daughter.

And bolted upright when the hand grasped his shoulder.

"Jerry? Jerry Blackwood? That you, mate?" Spoken with a thick Aussie accent and a little too much strength in the grip of the fingers.

It took a moment, but the lined, blue-eyed face pasted on the bald, bullet-shaped head gradually formed into someone he recognized, but bigger than he remembered. Older, too. But the years hadn't shrunken this guy's muscles any. It looked like he'd gone on steroids—or maybe it was his own paranoia talking. He swallowed.

Don't want to be tossing those shit-colored glasses just yet, big guy.

"Brian Jones. Now aren't you a sight for sore eyes. Or one to cause them."

Brian grinned, but the smile didn't reach his cold blue eyes. Without invitation, he pulled out the empty chair at Jeremy's table and sat down. His black t-shirt was pulled tight over his broad chest, and his light linen jacket wasn't loose enough to hide the bulging muscles—or the gun he wore. The waitress, a petite young thing with the usual short-shorts, midriff-baring top, and head of long black hair, hurried to the table.

"Singha, sweetie." He named an Indian beer and leaned back in his chair like a crocodile eyeing its prey.

Just how did a guy close to Jeremy's fifty-two years come off looking like he was barely forty?

Jones shook his head and studied Jeremy with those flat, reptile eyes. "How long's it been, mate?"

Jeremy shrugged. The man Jeremy had first met ten years ago when he had arrived in Phnom Penh had been one of those seemingly jobless men who knew everyone. In their brief association, Jeremy had come to think of Brian Jones as a 'fixer.'

You need drugs? He could get them.

You get arrested for drugs? He could help with that, too.

You need a new backpack? A gun? A girl? Insert here what it was you wanted—and Brian Jones was the man for you. Back then, Brian had been a hard-bitten man of indeterminate age, who'd traded on his physique and square jaw to impress the ladies. He'd also been a drinking buddy.

He definitely wasn't the person Jeremy wanted to meet tonight.

"Eight, nine years."

"Nah. Longer, I think, mate. At least ten."

Jeremy nodded. The conversation lagged, and Jeremy wished he was back on Sisowath instead of this backwater eddy of a place, because the stream of tourists would at least give him something to talk about.

And witnesses.

Brian jerked his chin at the canvas satchel. The neon reflected off his shaved head.

"You been busy, I hear," he said, the neon catching the skin around his eyes and revealing deeper lines that made him look older than the almost fifty years Jeremy had given him.

The waitress brought his beer and he met Jeremy's gaze and leaned across the table. "So you want to tell me about it? Enquiring minds and all that shit…?"

The wine soured in Jeremy's stomach, and he pulled his satchel onto the floor beside him, because no one should be hearing anything about what he'd been doing. Unless he'd seriously miscalculated.

"Who're you working for, Brian?"

Brian smiled his broad, predatory smile, exposing the gap between his teeth that, at the moment, looked like a deep cave. "Let's just say a businessman, and like any businessman, he knows a good investment when he sees it."

Brian's smile faded, and behind it lurked the ruthlessness that had helped him assume a role in Phnom Penh that had existed since the Portuguese and Dutch set up shop in the city in the 1600s. The role had reached its heyday during the Vietnam War, and had resurrected itself after Pol Pot's reign came to an end. Then, as now, men sold influence through violence, and Brian was their tool.

"No one's seen anything, Brian." Except the staff at the Ministry of Lands had seen his geological survey. His stomach sank and a bead of sweat ran out of his hair and down his temple. He swiped it away, but not before Brian saw.

Jeremy didn't want to talk about it. He didn't want to talk about it here—out in the open with the two older tourist women eating at the next table and congratulating themselves about how brave they were, eating off the main tourist strip.

He shoved his wine glass away, the tannins too sour on his tongue.

But then, maybe talking here with the women around was the safe way to go. Safety in numbers and all that.

He hauled his canvas bag onto his lap. Opened it and pulled out the least of the samples he'd taken and shoved it across the table at Brian. Brian covered it with his broad palm and then lifted his hand like he was uncovering cards.

Brown rock was what it looked like—until Brian turned it over. His eyes widened a little and he casually turned it over again, hiding the small, rough, red gems poking out of the grey-brown corundum.

He nodded. "Nice looking, mate. More where that came from?"

Jeremy gave a single shrug and hated that he did. If he were a stronger man, he'd just tell Brian Jones to get lost. Hell, if he were a stronger man, he'd never be here at all. But not being stronger, he'd find a way around Brian. He'd always found the words to talk his way through problems.

Well... most of the time.

Brian slipped the sample into his pocket without asking permission, and a chill ran down Jeremy's back, even in the sweltering heat. Brian smiled that crocodile smile again: *gonna eat you, mate*.

"Then it seems we got cause for celebration, don't we? Our new partnership."

He reached over and emptied the wine bottle into Jeremy's glass. "Drink up, mate. We got places to go, people to see. Then we're going t'get rich. *Together*."

No choice. *But you always have a choice, Dad*, Kaitlin would say. A choice and a plan.

He picked up the glass, knowing this time his daughter was wrong.

Chapter 1

June 1st, Phnom Penh, Cambodia

Typical. Dad *would* drag her into miserable weather. Of course, he'd dragged her into so many other dodgy situations that monsoons were probably the least of her problems.

Probably. Knowing Dad.

Kaitlin Blackwood hunched down Sisowath Boulevard. The monsoon deluge flooded the streets, pounded the sidewalk, and sent two-inch rivers running down the pavement and over her newly-purchased street hikers. It beat on the roofs and storefront awnings—and her head—like a drum. It pummeled the broad, silver river beyond the road so that the air filled with the cacophony of water on water that made her ears ring.

More filthy water poured in gushing torrents off rooftops and filled the air with the stench of wet dog and garbage. Come to earth it split into tributaries as she stubbornly dragged her overnight suitcase down the sidewalk-turned-river.

Another wave of street-water sprayed her. The damned taxis, motorcycles, and odd-shaped moto-taxis—motorcycles with small, covered four-seater trailers—belched exhaust as they plied their way up the river-nee-street. Their drivers' calls beat at her, as incessant as the pounding rain, "Taxi, miss? Taxi. It rain hard."

It was hard not to scream at them, but then she'd never been a screamer.

She straightened, determined to look like she knew where she was going. Yeah, it rained hard here. It rained hard in Seattle, too. Maybe not like this, but she was used to getting wet.

Of course, she had a Gore-Tex jacket there.

She tossed her head, but her mass of rain-blackened blond hair just slapped her in the face and plastered there. *Perfect. Perfect in every friggin' way, Dad. You are sooo going to hear about this. It's a good thing I love you.*

Her clothes—light t-shirt and denim capris—plastered to her, too, so the passport carry bag she wore under her clothes from a cord hung around her neck stood out like a third breast on her chest. But she was *not* taking a taxi.

It was one of the damned taxis that had deposited her at the dive of a hotel she'd spent last night at not-sleeping. They could just take her out and shoot her before she'd trust another one. In fact, she'd break her own rule—buy a gun and do it herself—before she'd trust anyone in this stupid country again.

Locals and tourists wore cheap, see-through rain slickers and dodged around her like the rain didn't matter. She'd buy one, but she was so soaked now, what difference would it make? Besides, buying one would require energy to communicate across the language barrier. Energy she didn't have.

She waded northward on Sisowath—at least she thought it was northward. As jet-lagged as she was, she wasn't sure of much except that the darned taxi driver had pointed this way along the street last night when she'd asked him about the address.

She looked down at the soggy note in her hand. Ink pooled on the paper and ran onto her fingers. By the numbers on the restaurants and bars and tourist shops, the place she was looking for should be right around here. At least she thought so. She paused for a moment, studying the numbers and wiping rain out of her eyes.

Yes, it should be.

A petite female shopkeeper wielded a broom to keep the water out of her trinket shop and a tidal wave rolled across Kaitlin's feet right up to her ankles.

Perfect. Just perfect. Kaitlin sighed.

The shopkeeper said something that might have been an apology, but then again it probably was more like get out of the rain you stupid woman, and while you're at it, get out of my country.

More than happy to. In fact, she'd be downright ecstatic.

If she could just find the darned address. And her father. Then she'd give him a piece of her mind and be on the next plane out of this stupid country. Cambodia. *Now I ask you?*

A tug on her suitcase turned her around and she found herself facing a man. Cambodian — she thought. Oriental at least. Five foot eight?

Shorter than her five foot ten, at least, and dressed in a khaki-colored shirt and trousers that even in this deluge looked pressed.

But his hand was holding the handle of her suitcase and all her internal alarms went off. Another taxi tout?

His black gaze met hers. And then he smiled, exposing a mouth of blackened teeth that made her skin crawl, but in a country like this, dental hygiene couldn't be what it was in America.

"You are lost, Miss? Perhaps I can help. Perhaps you need a hotel. Or a taxi."

Kaitlin jerked her suitcase a little closer, but the darned guy didn't release it. "I'm fine. Thanks. I'm just looking for an address, but it has to be near here."

"What is the name and I will help you?"

She rolled her eyes. Couldn't these guys figure out she wanted to be left alone?

"All right. I'm looking for the Mayview Hotel."

"Ahh, yes. That one. Is good, but not as good as my place. You have a look, okay?"

That blackened smile again, and it frankly turned her stomach, but she supposed the poor guy couldn't help it.

"It is on the way to Mayfair. Come."

She hesitated—but it would be good to get there and out of the rain. Finally she nodded. "The Mayview," she corrected.

"This way, please." He caught her wrist with strong fingers and started to lead her back the way she'd come.

"I've been that way," she said.

"Mayfair sit on different road and my place this way. We go my car."

She stopped. The internal alarms jangled again. Something wasn't right. "The address I have is for Sisowath Quay. And it's the Mayview."

"No. No. No. Mayfair — it move."

The blackened smile again, but his eyes didn't match.

"No. It move."

The lack of expression reminded her of a young Disciple gangbanger she'd interviewed for a story back home. The guy had come across as a psychopath in her estimation. And the story she'd written for the *Post Intelligencer* had earned her a credible enough death threat she'd had police checking on her for six months. The gang member had turned up dead in a prison hit not long after.

And this guy's eyes were just as dead to emotion. And now that she listened to her instincts, the cut of his clothing just didn't fit a tout. Or a taxi driver. It had a military cut to it.

She tried to ease her hand free. "I don't think I need any help, thanks."

He didn't release her.

Internal air-raid sirens klaxoned through her head. She tried to twist loose, but he didn't release her.

"Dammit, let go!"

He half-dragged her toward the street corner. If he got her off the Sisowath Quay, who knew what would happen. The question was what to do? All the self-defense training seemed to disappear.

So she kicked him.

His grip only tightened.

She could stomp on his foot if she could find it under all this water. She could slam the heel of her hand into his nose. She could....

"Bloody hell, mate. The lady doesn't look like she wants to go with ya."

A booming voice that was weirdly familiar, but then she was rattled. And the voice spoke English like a native speaker, even if it held a thick Aussie accent.

She ripped loose, grabbed her suitcase, and ran.

"Hey!" The Aussie voice she hadn't even thanked, but she needed to get out of here. Some place where she understood what was going on. A place where she could figure things out.

She splashed back the way she'd come. Past the hotels. Past the bars. Past the trinket shop where the woman had drenched her shoes. A set of clean stairs in a yellow-and-white painted building came up on her left. A brass sign read *Foreign Correspondents' Club*.

Well she sure was foreign. And a journalist.

She almost ran up the stairs, her suitcase bang-bang-banging behind her, and she hated the panic pounding in her chest. Not like her. Not like her at all, dammit.

She was cool. She was Kaitlin Blackwood, crime reporter, friend of district attorneys, lawyers, gang-bangers, and mob bosses alike.

It had to be the jet lag that left her feeling as fractured as some gothic romance heroine. And the fact that she hadn't planned for things like what had happened in the street. If you could plan things, you could be prepared.

At the top of the stairs waited a large open-air space with broad ceiling fans futilely turning the rain-soggy air that came in through the room's two open sides that overlooked the streets and the Tonle Sap River. A high counter ran the perimeter of the room to allow patrons to partake of the view, and the open space was filled with low tables and well-worn, low-slung chairs. An actual bar sat against the wall next to the top of the stairs, and a door to the rear gave a view of the rain-darkened tiered roofs of a magnificent building of ancient Cambodian structure.

She sank down into an ancient leather chair that smelled of years of cigarette smoke and spilled beer and dug her fingers into the scarred armrest. She closed her eyes and regretted the people moving around her. The darned migraine that had been coming on since just before her plane landed sat like a sniper just back of her eyes. If she didn't get some rest soon, it was going to catch her right in the forehead and then she'd be down for a day at least.

Another gift from her father dragging her half way around the world. She fumbled her note pad and a pencil out of her purse to make a new list.

"May I help you?"

She looked up to a slim young Cambodian man in a pale yellow uniform standing above her. Beyond him the huge ceiling fans churned the humid air, and outside the open-sided room, the sheets of rain still fell.

"Tonic water and lemon, please." The sun wasn't over the yardarm yet, so no booze, though, frankly, a little alcohol would probably go down good now. In the face of the neatly clad waiter, she tried smoothing her sodden shirt and capris, but only succeeded in sending a new runnel of water onto the leather chair and the floor. Drowned rat wasn't the half of it. Her hands were frigging shaking! But the voices of the people behind her were like hammers on pipes in her head, and booze was never good with a headache like this coming on.

"Very good." The server wandered away and she took a deep breath.

The restaurant/bar had none of the feel of her favorite haunts back home. No photojournalist's shots on the walls. No framed newspaper tear sheets. None of the feel of dust and dirt and old smoke and crime that went with most reporters' haunts. Instead, pale yellow walls held a few photos of Angkor, and to either side of her along the rail to the street, a few young tourists and a couple of older expats sat, singly and in small groups, getting quietly drunk.

But the low tables and leather chairs must have been a pretty nice spot to wait out the Vietnam War. For some. A view of the river and none of the bombs that fell on Saigon.

She shook her head. She never had understood the call of the wild that made people become foreign correspondents when there was so much to report back home. She looked back at her note pad, trying to decide where to start.

Find hotel. And find her father. Go home. Pretty basic. What else did she need?

The young server returned and smoothly plunked the drink amid the water marks on the low wooden table, then left without even a smile. Not exactly the kind of service she was used to, but at least a twist of lemon floated amongst the ice.

She sipped, and it was a godsend of cool in the overwhelming heat and humidity. She sweated, even though her clothes still stuck to her from the rain. And her hands had barely stopped shaking.

Darn it, what was going on with her? She'd had close calls before.

But none so far from house and home.

And home was what she was going to lose if she didn't find her dad and get home. Mac could only keep the publisher happy with guest columnists for so long, before they started thinking about giving someone else her column space.

And if that happened, her dad would have put her in a worse position than he had so many times before. She'd just dug herself out of the debt he'd put her in when, unbeknownst to her, he used *her* condo as collateral for a loan on a boat he'd decided he was going to sail to South America.

Of course, he'd sunk the damn thing somewhere off the tip of Baja and she was left paying. And paying. She picked up the bill for the tonic water. Three-fifty. Three-fifty flippin' U.S. dollars for a drink in this flippin' country with none of the comforts of home.

"And I'm still flipping paying."

"Well, if that's a problem, I s'pose I could help ya out. Can't have a pretty lady drinking with the flies, now can we? Course maybe she could buy me a drink fer helpin' her out...."

The suggestion came in thick rolling round vowels that were a tad thickened with liquor, but she was pretty sure it was the same voice she'd heard in the street. The voice of her savior and she shouldn't be ungrateful, but the slow Aussie drawl sent a jab of migraine pain right into her left eyeball. She refused to turn around, because making eye contact was where the trouble always began. Strangers could move right in on you and she really just needed to recover right now.

Out of the corner of her eye, a strong arm rested on the wooden arm of another of the worn leather chairs. Sun-bleached, blond hairs curled on its tanned and freckled back. Strong fingers curled around a sweating glass of beer. They were long. Almost artistic.

The kind of hand she always found attractive.

She looked away. Mac might not be her 'type,' but they were an item. He was a great guy. Stable. Just what she needed, not that she'd let it advance beyond dating. But she might.

Besides, Aussies were trouble.

"Thanks, but no thanks. But I'll buy you that drink for the help in the street. It was appreciated." She waved at the waiter and pointed at the Aussie's table without even glancing at it. There. Duty done. He should get the message.

Another sip of the tonic and the tension started to dissolve out of her shoulders. Too bad her clothes wouldn't dry just as fast.

"Yer lookin' a mite put out. Guy scared you, did he?"

Dammit, he wasn't going to let go and it wasn't true. She was capable. She didn't need saving. But he did deserve a thank you.

"Thanks, but I don't need any company. I'd prefer to be alone." She sipped her drink—well, maybe more of a gulp. Just finish and get out of here and find the Mayview.

"Now that's a sad tale, ain't it, lovely lady wants to be alone."

That was it. Enough, even if he'd helped her out. She turned her cold-blooded glare on him for an instant, then turned away.

"I *said*, no thank you." A slick of ice had crept into her voice.

"B.J., I think the lady wants to be left alone." A clipped British accent that seemed harsh after the lazy, rolling Aussie.

Thank you, lord. She almost looked at her defender, but something stopped her. Something he'd said. And her brief glance registered.

Oh-friggin-no....

She looked over again, into a boozy set of mocking blue eyes she had thought—no, make that hoped—never, ever, to see again.

To continue reading *Shadow Play* look for it at your favorite bookseller or go to ***www.twistedrootbooks.com.***

Mystery, Romance and High Adventure from Twisted Root Publishing

If you enjoyed this book, you might enjoy
other titles available from
Karen L. Abrahamson
in your local bookstore or wherever e-books
are sold.

Made in the USA
Middletown, DE
07 November 2021